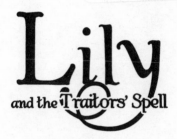

Lily
and the Traitors' Spell

'Unbind me,' Lily whispered. 'Free me...'

Her father held the water-flames dancing and licking around his hands, and lifted his cupped palms up to his mouth, pouring the silvery liquid down his throat and swallowing painfully in great tearing gulps. Then he dropped his hands, little silver dribbles running from between his fingers, and tipped slowly over onto his side, unconscious.

'What's happened?' Georgie cried, and she tore herself from the others and began to run towards him, but the dragon batted her aside with one massive claw.

Lily
and the Traitors' Spell

HOLLY WEBB

ORCHARD

ORCHARD BOOKS
338 Euston Road, London NW1 3BH
Orchard Books Australia
Level 17/207 Kent Street, Sydney, NSW 2000

First published in 2013 by Orchard Books

A Paperback Original

ISBN 978 1 40831 352 7

A CIP catalogue record for this book
is available from the British Library.

1 3 5 7 9 8 6 4 2

Printed in Great Britain

Orchard Books is a division of Hachette Children's Books,
an Hachette UK company.

www.hachette.co.uk

For everyone who wanted to know the end
of Lily's story

ONE

The bullet buried itself in the canvas backdrop with a solid thud.

Henrietta let out a yelp of surprise, flattening herself against the floor of the stage with her black eyes bulging.

'It's not meant to have proper bullets in it!' Lily gasped, turning to stare at Daniel, her fingernails digging into her palms.

It had been so quick. If the bullet had been about to hit one of her friends, she wasn't sure she would have been fast enough to stop it.

Argent, who had been sleeping draped across the back of the stage, shook out his wings a little, and blew out a thin, coiling breath of smoke. 'I have little experience with firearms,' he said, in a low, rumbling murmur. 'But that seemed quite real to me.'

Daniel was looking at the pistol, with a faintly puzzled expression on his face. 'It can't have been...'

'I hate this trick,' Nicholas muttered. He and Mary had only been working as Daniel's assistants in the illusionist's act for a few weeks, since they all returned from Fell Hall, but Nicholas swore to Lily that he had nearly died twice. Lily thought he was exaggerating, but perhaps not very much. Nicholas was ideal for the assistant's role, being very skinny and good at getting into tight places, but he had an awful memory, and that mattered when one had to be sure in which order very sharp knives were going to be stabbed through the cabinet one was hiding in. Nicholas had been trying to magic himself a sort of metal vest. He said it wasn't cheating, as the magic wasn't part of the trick, but no one else was convinced. Mary found it particularly irritating, as she had no magic of her own, and had to rely on getting it right the first time.

'Have you been messing with the pistol?' Lily asked Nicholas suspiciously.

Mary glared at him. 'I bet you have!'

'I didn't!' Nicholas protested indignantly. 'I honestly didn't! It isn't fair. Just because of that accidental green rabbit-creature, everyone always blames me.'

Daniel sat down rather shakily on the edge of the stage, laying the ornate, enamelled pistol down next to him. 'The rabbit still has a green tinge, Nicholas. And she's really gone off carrots. I don't like putting my hand in that hat any more, she bites.' He sighed. 'That wasn't a wax bullet, was it? What happened?'

Lily came and sat down by him, and Henrietta climbed shakily into her lap, one paw stretched across to Daniel's leg.

'I don't think this trick is a good idea,' Lily muttered. 'This time you were only testing the gun, but what if it happens again?'

'It won't.' Daniel tried to sound reassuring, but it didn't work very well. 'There must have been some sort of mix-up.'

Mary crouched down next to them. 'If that happened when I was firing it at you, I'd never forgive myself. And I don't see why this trick is so special anyway. It's stupid! Who would actually *want* to catch a bullet in their teeth?'

'But if it worked...' Daniel murmured wistfully. 'It's so dramatic...'

'It is quite dramatic when the back of your head is spread all over the stage, yes,' Henrietta growled.

Daniel got up, fetching the shallow box from the top of one of the cabinets. He lifted the lid with shaky fingers, and nudged the glistening black bullets, nicking them with his fingernails. 'These are real. All of them, apart from this one at the end.' He lifted it out, rolling it between his fingers. Then he pressed his forefinger to his lips. 'Sweet. And it isn't as heavy as the others. This is a sugar one, as they all should be.'

'Mystery solved then,' Henrietta snapped. 'Someone ate your sugar-coated bullets. One of the children.' She glared around at Nicholas suspiciously.

Daniel frowned. 'They aren't all sugar. Just a sugar coat over the wax – baked sugar, to look like metal, you know.'

Argent shook his wings with an anxious rattling sound, and came a little closer, stepping sinuously across the stage. 'Ah... The silvery-black things? The odd sweets, with the rather dull centre?'

Everyone turned to stare up at him, and he ducked his head, looking as embarrassed as a house-sized dragon possibly could. 'I do so like sweet things,' he murmured. 'So much nicer now than they were a few hundred years ago. There was marchpane, and liquorice root... But now! Mint humbugs! And chocolate... I could smell them – so delicious, and the colour so nice. I did put some of the others back in the little box, there was a bag, full of them...'

'Yes,' Daniel agreed grimly. 'The real bullets, for

showing to the audience.'

'Ah...'

'I should have noticed, when I loaded it,' Daniel muttered to himself. 'Perhaps we aren't ready for the gun trick – but it would get us so much publicity.'

'Banner headline. Tragic death of foolish illusionist,' Henrietta muttered.

'I really do apologise,' the dragon said, a flutey, breathless note sounding in his deep voice. 'I shouldn't have taken them. At least it was me that the bullet almost hit, in the end,' he added, snaking his neck down so that he could look up into Daniel's face. 'I'm sorry,' he said again, breathing out a gentle cloud of sparkling, filmy magic that wreathed itself around Daniel's face and shoulders like smoke.

Daniel sighed, and then took a breath in, shivering slightly as the magic shimmered through him, sending a silvery sheen across his skin. 'What did you do?' he murmured. He shook his too-long dark hair a little, as though he were shaking it out of his eyes, and it glittered. 'I feel stronger.'

'Mmm,' Argent agreed. 'It should last a while. I wanted to make it up to you. I should never have eaten them. But I have my doubts about this illusion, Daniel, my friend. Those thugs in the Queen's Men will never believe it's only a trick. Who could catch a bullet in their teeth *without* magic? They'll haul you off to prison – or they would if they had one, anyway.'

He allowed himself a smug little puff of smoke here. Lily and Georgie had broken into Archgate, the magicians' prison where their father had been locked away. They had not gone alone – Rose, one of the magicians who had set the original guardian spells, had led them through the traps she'd laid so many years before. They had also taken a princess with them – one of the few who could open the secret door, which was spelled to respond only to royal blood. It was pure chance, and luck, that the girls had a princess to hand, having rescued her and taken her with them when they escaped on dragonback from Fell Hall, a reform school for magician children. Princess Jane had been the oldest inhabitant, hidden away there when she refused to condemn all magic. She had been left to grow old in the attics of Fell Hall, while her loving subjects were told she'd died.

Even with a princess, and a magician to help them, Lily and Georgie had still been caught. The Queen's Men had attacked them, just as they had managed to rescue their father from the cell he'd been shut in for nearly ten years. Queen Adelaide, the Dowager Queen, hated all magic and magicians, after a magician had murdered her husband. She had been so determined to see them caught that she'd accompanied the guards to the prison, and she'd ordered her men to kill them all. When she woke in the night, Lily could still hear the old queen's hoarse, delighted voice, screaming gleeful orders as she saw what she had caught.

But Argent had sensed the danger they were in, and clawed and wrestled his way down the narrow passages and into the heart of the prison to rescue them. The guard spells had no effect on him at all – in fact, Lily thought they'd made him stronger. She was almost certain that somehow he ate magic. Which was good, as she wasn't sure what else he ate, and she didn't really want to know.

The prison had been left less than secure. The Queen's Men had put it about that a gang of renegade magicians had attacked the palace, as Archgate was hidden under the ceremonial arch that led into the palace courtyards. Lily had read out the newspaper articles about it to Argent, with disgusted comments, until he had pointed out that actually, she *was* a renegade magician, and now that she had Rose, and her father, as well as Georgie and himself, and Nicholas, however accident-prone his magic was, they were almost a gang.

Lily quite liked the idea.

* * *

Lily peered around the door, trying to see into the dark little room. Her father was asleep in there, on a pile of quilts and blankets. Or she'd thought he was. If she hadn't known, she would have sworn the room was empty.

She took a step backwards. The room *was* empty. She shouldn't be there, anyway... Blindly, she turned away from the door and tripped over Henrietta, who was sitting in the middle of the passageway, shaking her head crossly as though her ears were itching.

Lily yelped and stumbled, putting her hands out to try to keep from falling onto the dusty floor, and then let out a little gasp of relief as someone caught her with a grunt.

'Peter!'

He shoved her back onto her feet, holding her arms above the elbows, and frowning, as though he wasn't sure what had happened.

'I just stumbled – I tripped over Henrietta,' Lily said slowly. She glanced at him to make sure that he was looking at her to read her lips, but then she went back to staring at the dark doorway. It wasn't right, somehow... And where had Peter come from, just in time to catch her?

Moving in a sort of daze, she turned back to peer at the darkened doorway, stretching an arm across the opening.

Empty. Empty. Empty.

But it *wasn't*. She knew it wasn't. Slowly, as if she were swimming through a golden, sticky syrup, Lily raised the back of her hand to her mouth, and bit down hard on her knuckle. The sharp little pain cleared the sticky honey trails out of her head, enough to make her see what was happening.

'You were in there!' she told Peter accusingly, speaking loudly, her face pressed close up against his, so he couldn't fail to understand her. 'What were you doing? That's my father's room!'

Peter let go of her, stepping back and reaching for the notebook in his pocket. He held it between them, the stub of pencil hovering over the page, but he didn't write anything. He didn't know what to say. Eventually, he wrote, in a neat, small script – so much tidier than Lily's own untaught hand – *He can't talk either.*

'What did he say?' Henrietta demanded. 'Where is your father?'

'So – you were with him?' Lily asked, feeling almost hurt. She hadn't thought of their shared lack of speech as a bond between Peter and her father.

She had hardly spoken to him herself, since they had dragged him onto Argent's back and fled from Archgate. It had only been two days, and he needed to recover his strength. He was tired. Overwhelmed. They had understood, and left him to rest in that pile of quilts, bringing him food – the nicest they could afford. And newspapers. Henrietta had thought of those, in case he might like to know what was going on in the world, after ten years shut away from everything on his own.

Apart from that, Lily and Georgie had tactfully left him alone, just popping in to say good morning, and to bring him his meals. Because once she spoke to him properly, Lily knew that she wouldn't be able to stop. Questions would pour out of her, about Merrythought, and her mother; and, had he known about the spells that had killed their sisters? Had he let Mama set her evil spells in Georgie? Had he *wanted* her to?

And now that he had been set free, could he free Lily's sister too?

Lily had walked past his door so many times in the last few hours, each time forcing herself to keep on walking, to leave him till he was better, to accept that he was ill, and broken by his years in the prison...

Now it seemed that Peter had been talking to him all this time, and in secret, hidden by that cloaking spell.

Went to take his breakfast plates away, Peter scrawled in explanation. *He stopped me. Wanted to know stuff.*

'He's got a spell across the door, though,' Lily said,

frowning. That meant that her father was well enough to do magic – and that Peter had managed to get past the spell.

He did seem surprised I managed to get in, Peter agreed, after a pause. *I didn't know there was a spell.*

Lily looked him up and down. She'd known him for so long, ever since he'd been abandoned on the little stony beach at Merrythought, when they were both small. She tended just to think of him as someone who was always there. She had hated leaving him behind, after he'd helped them to run away from the island, and she'd begged him to come with them then. But Merrythought was the only home Peter had ever known, and he hadn't dared to leave it. He had shoved their tiny boat out onto the water, and hidden himself away under the jetty. She had looked back for him, but he was gone.

Now, even in the dim light of the passageway, she could see that he suddenly looked older. Perhaps it was the effect of the strange spells at Fell Hall. Magic was strictly forbidden now, of course, but there were certain exceptions. When Lily and Georgie had first been sent there, it hadn't taken Lily long to discover that the cocoa they were fed at bedtime was drugged with spells. Old, dried-out husks of spells, but still strong enough to dose up children. Especially as most of the children at the school had been falsely accused, some of them as babies, and they hadn't any magic anyway. The cocoa, and the drifts of binding spells wound around the buildings and the outer walls, had dulled most traces of magic in the children, but the staff still carried little blue glass bottles full of powdered spells, ready to squash any hint of rebellion.

The staff had been convinced that Peter was a witch-child, like Lily and Georgie, and his muteness had only seemed to make them more determined to break him. Even after Argent had cleared the minds of all the children imprisoned at Fell Hall, Peter had been so heavily drugged with spells that he hardly seemed to be there. They had almost lost him as he slipped bonelessly from Argent's back when they flew up out of the ruins of Fell Hall. One of the smaller, wilder dragons had caught him, but Lily still remembered that moment of horror, when she'd watched him spiralling lightly down through the blue air, like a leaf.

'Maybe magic doesn't work on you the same way now?' Lily murmured. 'After all those spells... Oh!' She turned, surprised, and clutched at Peter's arm. Henrietta was already trotting towards the doorway, her ears twitching frantically. Lily followed her, drawn by the sweetest spell she'd ever felt. She *wanted* to go into that room now. She had to. It would be awful not to...

'That's very rude,' Henrietta snapped, as she fetched up against the pile of blankets, staring crossly at Lily's father.

Lily was quite glad that Henrietta had said it, so she didn't have to.

'You could just have asked!' Henrietta said, in a muted growl.

He smiled, rather sadly, and shook his head.

'Oh, well, I suppose not...' Henrietta muttered. 'But still...'

Peter stepped towards the makeshift bed, holding out his notebook and the stub of pencil, but Lily's father smiled again, and waved it away. He closed his eyes for a moment – without their sparkling greenish-blue lights, he looked older, and paler, Lily thought – and then opened them, staring at the wall.

Lily turned to see where he was looking, and laughed.

There was a baby in the wall. Very small, very plump, and reaching out fat little hands to Lily. She was wearing a faded yellow dress, and Lily frowned suddenly, reaching out her fingers to touch it, before she remembered that the baby was only a picture. She knew that dress. No one had ever thrown anything away at Merrythought, and there had been a dress just like that in the old wooden chest that stood at the end of her bed.

'Is that me?' she asked excitedly, turning to look eagerly at her father.

He nodded.

Lily sat down shakily on his blankets, still staring hungrily at the laughing child. He *did* remember her, then. He remembered her as a happy baby, not as her mother thought of her, as a weapon, to be filled with magic, and set loose against the queen.

'I didn't know if you'd remember us...' she murmured.

An older child appeared behind the baby, and Lily swallowed painfully. Georgie could only be three, but already she had a worried, frightened look in her eyes, and she was nibbling at the back of her hand. Mama's lessons had started.

'Why didn't you stop her?' she asked angrily, glaring into her father's eyes. How could he have let their mother do it? He must have known, Lily thought. Even if he had loved Nerissa to distraction, he must have seen...

By the time Lily was born, her older sisters Lucy and Prudence were already dead. They had not been strong enough to withstand the poisonous spells their mother had dripped into them. Slowly, they had faded and their magic had weakened, until they were useless. Now Mama was relying on Georgie. Lily had never been wanted, although she might perhaps be useful as a spare. But she had not been needed. Georgie had survived, even if she hadn't flourished.

Lily could just remember playing with her sister, when she was very small. But by the time Lily was four, and Georgie was seven, her older sister was too busy to play. She spent her days in the library with Mama, hidden behind walls of books and strange magical instruments.

Lily had wished and wished that Mama would teach her too, but her magic had never shown itself, and Mama already had Georgie. Why would she bother herself with the spare child, especially as this last little girl had no talent?

It was that seeming lack of talent that had saved her; Lily knew that now. She had escaped the spells, and when she'd found out what was happening to Georgie, she and Henrietta had persuaded her sister to run away. They had escaped from the old house on the island, and their mother, but Georgie couldn't outrun the spells. They were inside her, and they were waiting, growing stronger in the darkness. Soon, Lily was sure, they would break out, and do – something. It made it worse that even Georgie didn't know what it was she was meant to do. Only that it was something dark, and awful, and it was meant to bring the magic back.

They had been brought up believing the story – that Georgie was the child who would put everything back the way it should be, with magicians no longer shamed and hidden. It was her destiny, and it had sounded like something beautiful and noble. It was so obviously right! But neither of the girls had known how it was actually going to happen until they had chanced upon a list of spells, tucked away in the back of a photograph album. The album had held fading pictures of their older sisters, the ones who hadn't survived Mama's training. When Lily and Georgie had seen the list of spells, they'd understood why. All of them had been cruel, murderous things, designed to kill, and from the notes their mother had written, they were aimed at someone in particular.

As they read them, the awful truth had become clear.

The only way to bring magic back to the country was to get rid of the person who had banished it in the first place. Lily had no proof, but she was almost sure that her sister was going to kill the queen.

Their mother was part of a conspiracy, a band of magicians who were plotting to assassinate the royal family and take over the government, returning magic to power thirty years after it had been outlawed. She was so devoted to the cause that she was willing to use her own child as a weapon. All of her children, one after the other.

The killing spells were difficult to learn, and even harder to control. Mama had given up on Lucy and Prudence ever mastering them – she had let the older girls die, or she had killed them herself, Lily and Georgie weren't quite sure. She was giving up on Georgie too, they had heard her say so. She planned to send her the way of her sisters, and begin to train the last child instead.

Lily.

After that, all they could do was run.

Lily stared angrily at the spell dancing over the faded plaster. A younger version of Peyton Powers stood behind the little girls now, his hand on Georgie's shoulder. Lily looked at him, seeing the smooth face, and the springing golden-brown curls that were so like her own, and let out a breath of a sigh, her anger draining away.

She wondered if her father thought he still looked like that. He probably hadn't seen a mirror since they'd dragged him out of Archgate. Now his curls were limp and greyed, and his face was tracked with lines and shadows. She could see the resemblance, but the man behind her was old.

'I loved her,' the younger version of her father said sadly. 'I didn't understand what she was doing. I'm sorry, Lily. I'm so sorry. I'll do anything I can to heal your sister.'

'She's *your* daughter!' Lily yelled, her fists clenching. 'You should be looking after her, not me!'

Her father shook, his eyes brighter with tears. 'I know. You should never have been left. I should have realised what Nerissa was trying to do to Georgie. What she'd already done, to our Lucy, and Prudence...' His voice grated and growled, as though the words were hard to say, even though the image on the wall was only a spell, and it could have spoken any way he liked. He reached out a hand to Lily, shyly stopping before he touched her. 'I shouldn't have been so stupidly noble. I refused to give up my magic, and I left you all.'

'Yes.' Lily sighed. 'But actually, I don't think I could give mine up either,' she admitted.

'I wish you had been brought up here, Lily,' her father told her, smiling sadly. 'Here in London, the way it was before. You would have loved it.'

'Was there magic everywhere?' Lily asked him, sighing.

He shook his head. 'No – and that was a mistake, I

think. We magicians were too proud, and we asked too much money for our spells. Magic was only a plaything for the rich, and those without money hardly ever saw it. How could we expect them to fight for us, after the king was killed, and we were suddenly the guilty ones? We had never allowed people close enough to love us.' He frowned out across the room, remembering, and the tired, old-looking man in the bed sighed angrily.

'But still, magic would have been all around you, Lily, from the very day you were born. You would have grown up with other magician children, and tried out your first spells together.' He chuckled to himself. 'I set fire to the drawing-room curtains once, trying to conjure up a fire sprite.'

Lily nodded, her eyes hungry. 'I wish it had been that way too,' she murmured. 'I do understand. I couldn't let my magic go. But Georgie would, in half a second.'

Her father's nose wrinkled in surprise, and Lily suddenly giggled. Georgie did that too.

'I know. She's the strangest thing. She'd rather sew.' Lily shook her head. 'And I think she'd be like that even if her magic worked properly. She says she never liked it.'

'But you do?' her father asked her hopefully, and this time he took her hand.

Lily nodded. 'I love it. I can't imagine not having it. It must have been wonderful, when you were allowed to use magic whenever you liked.'

'You don't use it now?' her father asked. He frowned wearily. 'How did you come to be here, Lily, in the theatre? I heard some of the stagehands talking about spells – magic on stage. I didn't understand what they meant. Magic is allowed in the theatre now? Is it safe?'

'It isn't real!' Lily chuckled. 'It's just very, very clever. Daniel designs the tricks – illusions, he calls them. Georgie and I were his assistants, before Mama's awful servant Marten found us. She was made out of magic, did you know that? I suppose you must have done.'

'Nerissa finished a construct?' Her real father's face paled, and the picture leaned forward, as though he might step out of the wall. The younger Georgie held onto the full skirts of his coat, as though the thought terrified her. Baby Lily only smiled, and chewed her fat fingers. 'I never thought she'd bring one alive...' he muttered.

Lily nodded. 'It must have been after you – left. There were at least two. The one she has now is a horrible parrot, or it was when we saw it. She took it with her, to New York. She's gone to find more magicians to join the plot against the queen,' Lily added, when she saw his frown of surprise. 'Everyone on the ship couldn't stand that parrot, but they all believed it was real.'

'She's grown stronger then. She tried so many times – I hated the things, but she was determined to make them work. It's old, old magic.' He sighed. 'Lily, you promise me there's no real magic in these tricks your friend does?' A rush of scarlet flooded across his bony cheeks, and the picture father gave an apologetic cough. 'I know I don't really have the right to ask you such things. I've been away too long. But I can't bear the thought of you being found out, and shut up somewhere like Archgate.'

He meant it. Lily could feel him shaking next to her, and his fingers were almost hurting her arm.

'I promise. They're all just made with cunning hiding places, and Daniel waving his arms around, and doing all sorts of clever little tricks so people aren't looking in the right place.'

'Timing is very important,' Henrietta added smugly. 'I have naturally excellent timing. Daniel hasn't been able to replace me, since we became too well known to be safe. We were in the newspapers, you know.'

Lily laid her hand over her father's bony fingers. 'Actually, I should think you could give Daniel some very good ideas. Would you talk to him about it?' She caught Peter's sideways, hopeful glance, and added quickly, 'With Peter too?'

The mute boy looked up at her, his eyes shining, and Lily smiled. She'd seen the careful little drawings at the back of his notebook, delicate diagrams of new cabinets, and clever electrical devices. They looked like death traps to Lily, but she would never have said so. And they had to be safer than trying to catch a bullet.

Her father's eyes were brighter, and he looked intrigued, as Lily seized Peter's notebook and shoved it into his hands, riffling through the pages to find the drawings.

Peter gave a little moan of horror, but Peyton Powers shushed him with an upheld hand, tracing the drawings admiringly, and nodding.

Then he looked up at Lily, and smiled. The strange, too-young figure on the wall said, 'Yes.'

Lily was sure she heard her father whisper it too. 'Esss...'

TWO

'You spoke!' Henrietta pointed out, climbing up his legs, so she could stare at him properly with her round black eyes. 'Will your voice come back, then?'

Lily hadn't wanted to ask him. She supposed that his voice had been taken, somehow, to make him less dangerous. That if he couldn't say 'magic words' he was less frightening. She was pretty sure that was nonsense. That those without magic didn't really understand how it worked. He was a very powerful magician – if he couldn't make a spell in his head, or with a few passes of his hands, there would be something very wrong. But it had definitely weakened him.

'One day...' The figure in the wall was fading as it

smiled, and the little girls were waving at her. 'Soon, I hope. Maybe you can help me. Must rest now.'

Lily nodded, and moved to get up, and leave him in peace. Then at the last minute, she darted shyly back to kiss his cheek, and he beamed wearily at her.

Come back soon...

Lily wasn't entirely sure how he had said it – in her head? Georgie had managed to speak to her silently once. Or was it just the remnants of the spell on the wall? She knew she had heard him, anyway. He had spoken to them like this in the rush of magic around the rescue, but Lily hadn't realised the magic would carry on.

What shall we do to help him? Peter scribbled in his notebook as they stopped in the passageway outside. *Why can't he speak?*

Lily frowned, and hesitated. She felt a little odd discussing it with Peter, since he couldn't speak either. When he had been abandoned as a child, the servants at Merrythought had tried to get him to tell them who he was, but he could neither speak, nor hear them asking. That was why his family had left him, Lily had assumed. They were frightened of his silence. They had thought he would fit in on the island of strange magicians.

JUST SAY! he scrawled, in cross, untidy capitals. It

was his way of shouting.

'It must have been a spell,' Lily told him, being careful to look at him, and shape the words properly. 'But something very strong, or maybe just very unusual. If he can still make illusions like the one he just showed us, he can't have lost his magic, or not all of it anyway. And the guard spell, on his room! That was really clever. So only a very powerful spell would work on him, don't you think?'

Peter nodded thoughtfully, and then grabbed her hand, dragging her back along the passage towards the stage. With his free hand he made a sort of flapping motion, and Lily nodded. He was right – they needed Argent. The dragon knew all kinds of strange little scraps of magic. There was no telling what he might come out with. He probably did have a spell for restoring stolen voices, if only he happened to remember it at the right time. Lily didn't think his great age was making him forgetful, it was more that he had so many hundreds of years' worth of memories and magic, all bound up together. Sometimes he had trouble untangling the bit he wanted.

But at the edge of the stage, they pulled up short. Argent was there, of course – he didn't fit easily into many other parts of the theatre, so he tended to stay draped decoratively across the back of the stage. When he wasn't wanted for a scene, a plain drape was let down to shield him from the audience, and when the drape was lifted, he did a remarkably good imitation of an automaton, lifting his head in stilted, clockwork twitches, and allowing the very thinnest column of smoke to spiral out of his nostrils. The scene painters were extremely proud of him, and several of them polished him daily. They had been photographed standing in front of him for a stage paper, and a number of them had been offered money in the local dives, by rival theatre companies after the secrets of his manufacture. Luckily, the dragon's obvious ability to burn to a crisp anyone who blabbed had stopped them all talking – combined with his own particular charm.

Argent wasn't alone. He was stretched sleepily out on the wooden boards with his head resting on his front legs, rather like an enormous dog. His eyes were half lidded, as he watched his companions, who were all seated on a long velvet cushion which had been placed along the end of his tail, turning it into an unusually scaly bench. Lily's sister Georgie was curled up next to Princess Jane and Rose, the elderly magician they had brought back with them from New York. In her day, she had been one of the most powerful magicians in the country, part of the ancient Fell bloodline, which Lily and Georgie and their father were distantly related to as well.

Lily and Peter stared at them in disgust. They were sewing, of all the stupid things. Princess Jane almost always had a delicate little embroidery basket with her – it was all the princess had taken with her when the girls rescued her from Fell Hall. Georgie and Rose seemed to be working on a dress, quite a plain one, so it must be for Georgie, or maybe even Lily herself. The theatre costumes were always covered in spangles and feathers and never, ever came in a sensible shade of middling grey.

'Sewing, again.' Henrietta snorted quietly. 'What a waste.'

Rose's familiar, the large white cat Gus, glanced up, and yawned at Henrietta, showing quite as many teeth as the dragon, though admittedly his were smaller.

'So rude!' Henrietta hissed. She was very jealous of Gus, who had been a familiar for a great deal longer than she had, and made sure she knew it.

'Are you all right?' Georgie asked, looking up at her anxiously. Lily and Peter were practically seething with impatience, and they looked most put out.

'Yes. We wanted to talk to Argent.' Lily frowned. 'But actually, Rose...' She still found it hard to call her that. The older magician was so famous. 'You might know too,' she added shyly. It was, after all, what they had gone all the way to America to fetch her for. She had helped to set the spells on the prison where their father was held, and the girls had been desperate to free him. Not only for his own sake, but for Georgie's.

Lily looked critically at her sister, as she set delicate stitches in the grey fabric. Georgie was paler and thinner than ever. Since they had encountered their mother on board the steamship, and then in New York City, the spells she had put into Georgie were wakening again. Lily was convinced that Georgie was having to fight against them all the time now, although she wasn't sure if Georgie knew that too. The dark magic had been part of her sister for so long that she kept the spells buried inside her without a conscious effort.

It meant that she could never use her own magic now, without releasing those darker spells. She had used them, a few times, when they had been a last resort. But each time they were harder to shut away, and in New York, so close to their mother, who had cast them, they had almost overpowered Georgie, leaving her faint and sick.

Lily had been sure that their father would know how to remove the spells – it was his own wife who had set them, after all. And Georgie was his child. He had to be able to.

But only if he recovered, and surely the first step was to bring back his voice.

'It's Father,' Lily began, and Georgie glanced up at her sharply.

'Is he any better? I looked in on him this morning – or at least, I think I did...' She frowned.

'Better enough to have set a very complicated guard spell on his room. You probably meant to visit him, and then you remembered something terribly important that you had to do instead.' Lily smiled. 'But the funny thing is, it didn't stop Peter.' She nudged his arm to show him she was talking about him. 'I'm wondering if he might be immune to some magic now, after recovering from all those spells at Fell Hall.'

'It's possible,' Argent murmured, lifting his head, and sniffing interestedly at Peter. Peter stood very still, and tried to look as though it wasn't worrying to be sniffed by a house-sized mythical beast. 'How intriguing. Sit here, boy, so I can look at you properly.'

'Sit on him. On his leg, look.' Lily pushed Peter closer to the dragon. Since Argent didn't speak in any human fashion, and didn't have lips, Peter couldn't understand what he was saying.

Peter cast a panicked look at Lily, but did as he was told, sinking hesitantly onto Argent's foreleg, so that the dragon could stare into his eyes.

'What about Father?' Georgie asked impatiently. 'What's happened, Lily?'

'He's starting to speak again. Not properly – he used a spell, making figures on the wall of his room. But then he *almost* spoke, I think. I heard him in my head. I'm almost certain he will be able to talk, one day. If only we could break whatever it is that's stopping him, then I'm sure he'd recover more quickly. And then...' She ducked her head, trying not to look at Georgie too hopefully.

'They're getting stronger every day,' Georgie murmured, gazing down at her sewing. 'I think Mama is on her way back from America. The spells can feel her getting closer. And we don't know what's happening with the rest of the plot. The Dysart girls, and any others there are, who have these same spells. I – it sounds strange, but part of me wants to go and find them all...'

'You see,' Lily said miserably. 'We haven't got long to free you, before those spells start doing whatever it is they were meant for. We *must* get Father better.'

'So we need a spell to release a bound tongue...' Rose said slowly. 'It must be a strong enchantment, though, to hold someone like your father.' She smiled at Lily's surprised face. 'I've met him, Lily, when he was a young student. He was most promising –

although rather...' She stopped, smiling apologetically.

'What?' Lily and Georgie asked together, intrigued.

Rose shrugged delicately. 'Just the teensiest bit stuffy?'

Gus sniggered.

'He had very strong principles.' Rose sighed, and gazed seriously at the two girls. 'Many people were surprised, you know, when he married your mother. He was deeply in love with her, everyone agreed. But they were so different – even then, she was known as someone who was not afraid to venture into... Well.' She shrugged, clearly trying to think of a nice way to say it. 'The less pleasant forms of magic.'

'He wouldn't give his magic up,' Lily said proudly. 'He may have been stuffy, but he wouldn't let it go.' She sat down next to Rose with a little sigh. 'And that meant he left us behind with Mama.'

Rose nodded. 'Exactly... Poor man. He can't have known. Or maybe he didn't want to know.' She sighed.

'So, do you know a spell?' Lily glanced between Rose and the dragon. 'A spell to undo another spell?'

'Water and fire,' the dragon rumbled, still weaving his head around Peter in fascination, and not really listening.

'What?' Lily asked sharply, and Argent blinked slowly at her.

'Water and fire – they'll undo most spells, if you use them right.'

Rose was nodding, but Lily found it hard to believe that something so important could be that easy. 'Really?' she asked doubtfully. 'Just any fire and water? What would we have to do with them? Nothing – nothing that would hurt him?' she added, suddenly anxious. Dragons were probably a lot less worried about fire than people.

Argent gave Peter one last thoughtful look. 'Tell the boy he is very lucky, Lily. I think – I'm not sure, but it seems so to me – that the way he has trained his mind and taught himself to see words made those spells at Fell Hall work on him more strongly than they did on anyone else. But now that he has fought against those spells and won, it would take a huge amount of magic to affect him. Really most interesting.' He waited while Lily explained to Peter, nodding approvingly, then all at once his attention seemed to switch to her question. 'Not any fire. A magical fire, Lily. One created from a very complex and difficult spell.' He drooped his head down to her and shuddered, smoke coiling out of his nostrils in little puffy clouds. It looked very strange, but Lily was almost sure that he was laughing. 'Or of course you could just ask me nicely.'

'Your fire could break the spell?' Lily flung her arms

around his muzzle without thinking, and then stepped back with a gasp. 'Sorry...'

'Not at all, not at all...' It was hard to tell again – the dragon's face was so very different from a human's – but Lily thought he was actually pleased. 'Dragons consume magic, in many different ways. We are very good at destroying spells, even strong ones.'

'What about the water?' Georgie asked. 'Does that need to be special too?'

Argent nodded slowly. 'It does, and that changes depending on the spell, and the person who has been bespelled.' He lowered his muzzle onto one foreleg, thoughtfully, and nudged at Peter with the side of his head, nearly knocking the boy to the floor. 'Tell him to scratch my scales. Just where his arm is. Helps me think.'

'He wants scratching,' Lily muttered to Peter, who blinked, but did as he was told.

'Ahhh. Mmm, yes. Most helpful. For your father, I should say perhaps you would want seawater – from the coast around his ancestral home, the island,' the dragon suggested.

'We have to go back to Merrythought?' Georgie cried, her voice full of horror.

The dragon shrugged massively. 'One suggestion. There may be others.'

'I have one...' Rose said slowly, and the girls stared hopefully at her. 'When I knew your father, he was a student, living in lodgings. A strange old building, a court, built around a cobbled square, with a fountain in the middle. Fountain Court, it was called. Between here and the palace. It was always full of student magicians. The fountain changed colour at least once a week, or ran with beer, or spouted fish... Is it still there?' she added, looking over Lily's shoulder to Daniel, who'd walked onto the stage to direct the stagehands in the hanging of a new backdrop.

'Fountain Court? It's not a place I'd want to live, but it's there,' he agreed doubtfully. 'I suppose after the Decree, the magicians moved out. After all, if you lived *there*, it was as good as saying you were magical, wasn't it?'

'Who moved in?' Georgie asked, in a small voice.

'People that nicely-brought-up young girls do not need to know about,' Princess Jane said primly, and Lily sighed. She wanted to know, but then, she hadn't really been brought up at all.

'So there you are,' Argent said, nodding hugely. 'You two should go, and fetch the water. That matters too.'

Daniel fetched an old envelope out of his waistcoat pocket and started to draw a map, but Lily looked at

Georgie uncertainly. The strangeness of the spells inside her made Georgie reluctant to leave the theatre, especially when someone always seemed to start chasing them if they went outside. 'Mama's still in America, as far as we know. Or maybe on her way back, but I don't think she's in London.'

Georgie gave a fragile, glass-sharp laugh. 'So, only the Queen's Men are after us then. And maybe the Dysart girls.'

'Yes...' Lily sighed. Cora and Penelope Dysart lived next door to their mother's sister, Aunt Clara. She had discovered the girls at the theatre, recognising them by Lily's resemblance to her mother. She had taken them to live with her, shocked by their appearance at the theatre, and terrified that somehow her fashionable London friends would find out that she had been born into a magical family. Aunt Clara had told herself that she had given up magic for so long that she even believed it herself, despite the hundreds of tiny glamour spells that curled her hair, and reddened her lips.

Aunt Clara spent a great deal of her time angling for an invitation to meet her neighbour, Jonathan Dysart, one of the queen's closest advisers. She was hoping that somehow he would provide her with a chance to visit the palace, and she had gleefully invited his twin daughters to meet Lily and Georgie.

It had taken less than a minute for the two sets of sisters to recognise each other for what they were, and scarcely longer for the Dysart girls to start plotting against these rival magicians. It was through their schemes that Lily and Georgie had been denounced and sent to Fell Hall. Jonathan Dysart had no choice but to send them. He had worked for years to build his place among the queen's courtiers, so that one day he could strike against her and help to overthrow the royal family, and bring magic back to power.

'I'll go without you, if you want,' Lily offered.

Georgie stood up, the grey dress slipping off her knees unheeded. 'I'm not quite that useless, thank you!' she snapped. 'Whatever that dog says!'

Henrietta was taken by surprise, and gawped at Georgie, her round eyes popping out even more than usual. 'I didn't say anything!'

'You were about to. Come *on*, Lily.'

'Maybe it's the spells making her grumpy,' Lily whispered, as Georgie stalked off to fetch her wrap, and Henrietta stared after her, looking most affronted. 'Do we need anything special?' Lily asked Argent, as she started across the stage to follow Georgie. 'Any special spell ingredients, or anything like that?'

'You *are* the ingredients,' he rumbled. 'Your father's daughters. Say a few words when you reach the fountain, that's all. Explain to the magic what you need. And a bottle would be useful.'

Daniel hurried into the wings, and came back with an armful of earthenware ginger beer bottles. He was always complaining that the stagehands left them lying around. 'Would these do?'

'She only needs one,' the dragon pointed out. 'These smell most delicious. Fiery, and spicy. What is this ginger beer?'

Lily left Rose explaining it to him and to the princess, who claimed she had never had it, as it was one of those things that were not readily available in palaces, along with gobstoppers. She hurried after Georgie, who was waiting by the little side door that the stage crew and performers most often used. It led out into a grubby alleyway down the side of the theatre, not at all like the smart stone frontage.

'Be careful, won't you!' Daniel called, leaning out of the doorway after them. 'It's not exactly smart round there. Are you sure you don't want me to come with you?'

Georgie looked hopeful, but Lily shook her head. 'I think it's supposed to be just us. We're the ingredients, like he said.'

'All right.' He shrugged. 'I'm coming after you if you aren't back in an hour or so, though. And watch your pockets!'

'Does he think I'm not going with you?' Henrietta muttered as they walked down the alley. 'I'd like to see a pickpocket get past me.'

'Dogs don't have pockets.' Lily giggled, in a silly, worried sort of way, and the pug dog glared at her coldly.

'You really shouldn't try to make jokes, Lily, it isn't your strong point. Some of us are not natural performers.'

'Sssh,' Georgie hissed, snatching the map from Lily. 'Come on. I just want to get there quickly.'

They were out onto a main street now, and Lily put her arm through her sister's, seeing the way she shrank back from the people passing by.

'No one can see what we are,' she whispered encouragingly, but Georgie shivered.

'I feel as though they can. Those spells are screaming in my head now, Lily, and they're so loud it feels as if everyone must be able to hear them.' She swallowed, her fingers digging tightly into Lily's arm as a horseman trotted past. His black uniform contrasted oddly with the snowy whiteness of his beautiful horse, and several other people in the street looked up at him angrily. An elderly man in a smart frock coat even shook his silver-tipped walking stick when the horse kicked up mud, splashing it over his shoes.

'See. Not everyone likes them, Georgie. It isn't only us scared of the Queen's Men. And people are daring to say it, now. I'm sure that's changed, even in the couple of months since we first came to London. The Queen's Men are too harsh, and they're making everyone remember the old days.' She sighed a little, remembering the way their father had talked about the magic in the city. Surely people wanted that again, that sense that magic was always just around the corner?

'I still think they'd inform on us, if they knew,' Georgie murmured, her eyes flicking anxiously from side to side, scanning the street. 'Don't you dare talk, Henrietta. Is that lady staring at us?'

'No. See, she's just looking for a shop. The hatmaker's, there. Stop worrying. Is it here we have to turn?'

They were heading out of the fashionable part of town now, leaving the smart shops and theatres for narrower, grubbier roads. The buildings were older, and thinner, and a great deal dirtier, and Henrietta snapped hungrily at a rat that ran in front of their feet and disappeared into a pile of rubbish by a doorway. She scuttled back in surprise when the rat darted its head out and snapped back at her, before whisking round, its horrid ridged red tail flicking back under the rags.

'It's awful here,' Georgie whispered. 'Are we close, Lily? Please? I want to get the water and go.'

'It ought to be just along here,' Lily muttered, turning the map in Georgie's hands a little, and glancing along the street. 'It's hard to tell, there aren't any street signs. But I suppose we'll know, we'll see the fountain.'

'*If* it's still there,' Henrietta growled. 'Don't start,' she added. 'There's no one close.'

'Daniel said it was,' Lily reminded her. 'Look for the inn with the painted fish. Oh, there, see!'

'Is that it?' Georgie said doubtfully, staring up at the sign above the lopsided old building. It creaked dolefully to and fro, and it might once have been painted with a fish, though now it was more of a silvery smear.

'And there's the courtyard!' Lily said, sounding relieved. The buildings around here looked so rickety that she wouldn't have been surprised if Fountain Court had fallen down since Daniel saw it last.

'Look at *them*!' someone said, and Lily glanced round anxiously, to see a gang of smaller children playing some sort of chase around the broken stone bowl in the centre of the courtyard.

'Aren't they grand?' one of the others laughed, and Lily glanced down at herself in surprise. She wasn't very smartly dressed, just in an old frock that Georgie had made over from something thrown out of the wardrobe. She hadn't even bothered with her cloak, although Georgie had fetched her a hat and gloves from their room. Living with Princess Jane, and even more so with Maria, who ran the theatre wardrobe, had given Georgie strict notions on what was proper for young ladies. Gloves were essential.

The children by the fountain had surely never owned any. Most of them were dressed, although the littlest boy, scarcely more than a baby, seemed only to be wearing a shawl tied around his middle.

'Proper fancy,' the oldest girl said disgustedly. 'What do you two want? If it's missions, we aren't interested. Not unless there's food. Is there? I don't mind a prayer meeting, if there's food after. Or first,' she added, with a sneer, and all the others laughed.

'It isn't missions...' Lily said slowly. She hadn't really thought about there being other people round the fountain. How were they going to explain taking the water?

'So? What do you want then?' the tall girl asked abruptly, hauling the shawl-wrapped boy off the stone lip of the fountain, before he fell into it.

Lily took a breath, trying to feel the magic inside her, to make herself braver. There were more children now, hurrying out of the doorways around the courtyard to join the crowd, and a few of their mothers too, glaring at her.

Lily wrapped her arms around the stoneware bottle, concentrating on her magic, and imagining the bottle full of the fountain water, all they needed to cure her father. 'Water. We only want some water,' she said, rather huskily, forcing herself to take a step towards the fountain. She could feel Henrietta pressed firmly against the side of her leg, a solid warm body pushing her on.

'Water? What, from this?' The girl laughed disgustedly, and the others joined in. 'Are you stupid? Look at it!' She drew back a little, letting Lily and Georgie see the fountain properly for the first time, and Lily let out a little gasp of disappointment.

The fountain was still there – with even a broken, stained little statue of a child, pouring water from some sort of vessel. Maybe something to do with magic, Lily thought miserably, as this had been a magicians' haunt. But it was dry, not even a trickle of water in the chipped stone jug, and the statue child looked blind and sad.

'No...' Georgie cried miserably, shoving her way

forward, pushing the older girl out of the way. 'No, we need it!'

'Hey...' The girl was obviously so surprised that this soft-looking rich girl had dared to barge past her that she hesitated, just for a breath. And then one of the others pulled her back, pointing.

'Look at her!'

'Georgie, don't...' Lily whispered, but it was too late. Georgie couldn't hear her now. Lily watched her sinking to her knees against the fountain bowl, one arm trailing into the water that should have been there.

And then it was. It seemed to rush into Fountain Court from all around, out of the air, as though Georgie's magic had stolen it from buckets and pumps, and pretty crystal glasses. It sparkled and gleamed as it rushed through the sky in diamond droplets, like rain, but sideways, and then even up, out from between the cobbles, bringing a rush of hair-thin grasses with it, and wiry little town flowers, all growing towards the fountain.

The younger children laughed, and one of the little girls spun round with her arms outstretched, catching the drops on her dirty jacket, so that she glittered like a grubby princess.

'She's a magician!' one of the boys muttered, looking sideways towards the entrance to the courtyard.

'One of them weird ones. We oughter tell.'

'Oh, please...' Lily turned to the older girl. 'Don't. We only want a little of the water, and we'll go. Don't tell them!'

'Will it stay?' the girl demanded suspiciously, nodding towards the water, which was trickling gently out of the stone jug now.

Lily nodded. 'I think so. It doesn't look like it's stopping, does it?' She knelt down anxiously beside Georgie. She was actually more worried that the magic wasn't going to stop. Georgie hardly had any control over it, and last time she'd let it loose out in the street, an enormous spell-wolf had nearly eaten them. 'You'd better get the rubbish out of the bowl,' she added. 'Her magic isn't very practical. She won't have cleared the drain, or anything like that.'

'Hmph.' But the girl nodded, and pushed a couple of the boys toward the fountain. 'You heard her. She leaned down to look at Georgie. 'Is she all right?'

'No.' Lily patted Georgie's cheek. 'No, she isn't. Her magic's gone wrong. That's what we need the water for, to help cure her.' She dipped her hand under the trickling jug, and cupped a little water in her palm, splashing it over her sister. 'Georgie, wake up. Please.' The water glittered as it ran down Georgie's pale cheek, and Lily licked her fingers thoughtfully. 'It's good water...' she murmured. 'Sweet. Very clean.' She fed a drop to Henrietta, who licked at it eagerly, and then shook her head, flapping her ears briskly, and put her front paws up on the basin, scrabbling to get her tongue towards the water.

At once several of the children reached over to do the same, filling their hands with water, as though now they'd seen Lily and the dog drink, they trusted it not to turn them into something dreadful.

The girl next to Lily stretched out her hand, and held the tiny puddle of water for the boy on her arm to drink. He sucked at it greedily, and reached out his own thin little hands for more.

'Thanks,' the girl muttered. 'Do you want us to help you carry her somewhere? She can lay down upstairs, in our room, if you like.'

'No, look...' Lily murmured. The water she had splashed onto Georgie's face had trickled down into her mouth, just a drop or two, and her lips had reddened again.

'Give her some more,' the girl suggested, reaching her hand under the fountain, and offering Lily a handful of water.

Lily nodded, and the girl dripped it slowly into Georgie's mouth, nodding approvingly as she saw Georgie lick her lips. 'Whatever she did, we won't tell.

There isn't a pump near here that works, not till two streets over. And it doesn't taste like this. She's opening her eyes.'

Lily glanced down, and saw that she was right. Georgie was looking up at them vaguely, and Lily hugged her, wrapping her arms around her sister hard. 'Look what you did,' she told her, half-crossly.

'Oh...' Georgie struggled up a little, gazing at the sunlight shining through the water. 'I didn't – it didn't do anything bad?' she asked anxiously.

'Not yet,' Henrietta muttered very quietly from by her feet.

'No. Here, take the bottle. I think you should do it.' Lily handed her sister the ginger beer bottle, and watched as Georgie held it under the fountain, hearing it gurgle and fill, like the water was laughing.

THREE

*Y*ou did this for me? Lily's father scribbled, stroking the bottle with his other hand, and smiling shyly at them.

Lily nodded. 'Georgie's magic. She made the fountain work again, it's beautiful.'

I can feel it, there's sunshine in the water. His letters came out straggly with strange loops and spikes here and there, from lack of practice. Lily wondered if his voice would be the same, when they brought it back. *Are you all right, Georgie?* he wrote carefully, holding out the pad to her with a worried look. *The magic didn't hurt you?*

Georgie looked down at her hands, as though she didn't quite believe they were hers. 'No – perhaps it was just glad to be out...' She shivered. 'But it was hard to wake up. I could feel Lily calling me, and the other children staring, but I was all wrapped up in the spells.'

'The water woke you,' Lily said, nodding at the bottle. It seemed to glow a little, in the dark room, and it made the air smell sweeter.

A good omen, their father wrote. *A sign.*

Lily nodded. She wasn't sure who the sign was from, but she would take it anyway. They seemed to have been chasing about for such a long time. From Merrythought, to London, to Derbyshire and back. And then to New York to ask Rose for help. Each time they thought they were a little closer, and then suddenly a whole new part of the road would open up in front of them. Surely it was time for the spells to start unravelling. They'd worked so hard.

'So will you get up?' she asked hopefully. 'Can you? Argent – the dragon, you know – he says he can provide the fire, to dissolve the spell, but he won't fit down here.'

Her father pushed the blankets aside, and swung his legs slowly to the edge of the mattress. He was still wearing the tattered shirt and trousers that he had arrived in two days ago, and he brushed his hand over the trousers wearily, and glanced up at Lily and Georgie, his eyes half mournful, half laughing.

Lily laughed back, her heart suddenly beating harder. It felt like a joke, a shared joke, the sort of thing she would have with Georgie, or Henrietta. *Look what the cat's dragged in.* A family thing. He had missed so much of their lives that it seemed even more special.

Georgie smiled triumphantly, and laid the folded bundle she'd been carrying onto the bed next to him. 'It's for you. I asked one of the girls in the wardrobe to get it for you.' She gave him a sudden worried look. 'It's from the rag market, it's a bit old and faded... I mended the holes...'

But he smiled at her, and reached up to stroke her cheek, before unfolding the bundle and revealing a dressing gown. It had once been a grand, showy garment, in dark red brocade, with satin lapels, but it was faded now to a streaky rose colour, and it smelled faintly of ancient cigar smoke. Standing up shakily, he pulled it on, and the long heavy folds swished around him like a robe. He looked stronger, and younger, without the torn and greyish shirt, and he laughed to himself as he tied the black cord around his waist and buried his hands in the full sleeves.

He tucked the little notebook – one of Peter's – and the stub of pencil in the deep pocket, and reached out his hands to Lily and Georgie.

Lily slipped her hand in his, feeling the thin bones

under her fingers, and the dry, papery skin of a prisoner kept without light.

Her father squeezed her hand gently, and smiled down at her, as though he knew what she was thinking. Lily pressed close against him, enjoying the feeling of being small – of having a father, of having someone else to be in charge. Even if he was sick, and couldn't speak to her.

Lily and Georgie led him slowly through the passageways up to the stage, and he blinked nervously as they came out of the wings and into that bright, busy space. Lily was so at home there by now that she had to stop, and try to see it as he did, with people scurrying here and there with odd bundles, and piles of rope, and paint pots. A group of jugglers were arguing with each other over the gaslights at the front, and as they walked out of the wings Henrietta started hissing at the performing poodle that Daniel had foolishly engaged.

And of course, there was a dragon stretched out along the back wall, apparently asleep. He opened one large, dark eye, though, as they came closer.

'Did you find it?'

Peter and Daniel, who had been putting a new coat of paint on one of the illusion cabinets, jumped up and came over to see, both looking relieved.

Lily pointed triumphantly to the bottle weighting down her father's dressing-gown pocket. 'Georgie did it. It's beautiful water, it tastes sweet, and it's so clear. I know all water's clear, but this glitters.' She dug her nails into her palms anxiously. 'I'm sure it's right.'

Her father gently let go of their hands, staggering just a little as he balanced himself, and then he pulled the bottle out of his pocket, offering it to the dragon.

Argent reached out one massive front foot, turning it sideways so that the bottle could be placed inside a cage of claws. 'Mmmmm,' he murmured admiringly. 'I can feel it. Alive, almost.' He closed his eyes for a moment. 'Ah, good. She's coming.'

'Who? Rose?' Lily asked, her eyes widening. 'Can you call people like that?'

'Of course. She's a Fell, Lily. And you know I can, child; I called you, did I not? I summoned you at Fell Hall. I could feel your magic, and I needed you to help me wake. The Fell blood is in you two, and your father, I told you that. Distantly related, but still. Enough for us to need each other.'

Rose hurried onto the stage, with Gus wrapped round her shoulders like a fur tippet. 'Did you...? I heard someone. That was you, wasn't it?' she demanded, staring at the dragon. 'You could be a little more polite!'

Argent ducked his head, gazing at her through half-lidded eyes. 'So sorry. I am out of practice. I will be more fulsome next time.'

Gus slid sinuously down to the stage, and stalked over to glare up at him. 'Good. I heard it too, and cats do not respond to *Come*! I am not a dog. Thank goodness.'

Henrietta snarled, and Lily crouched down to hug her. 'Just ignore him. You know he's doing it on purpose.'

'Of course I know.' Henrietta laid her ears back. 'It doesn't make him any easier to take.'

The dragon drummed his claws on the stage, a sharp volley of tapping, and then stared meaningfully at the bottle. The stopper began to turn gently, and then tumbled out. Lily was sure that the water inside was glowing faintly. She could see a shimmer above the open neck of the bottle.

'What do we have to do?' she whispered. She had never taken part in a ritual like this, a complex spell with so many magicians.

'Dear one.' The dragon gestured to Rose. 'You know the spell, do you not? I should be most interested to hear if it has changed, since my time.'

Lily suspected he was being extra flowery, to make up for his rude summoning before.

Rose nodded. 'I do know it, although I've never used dragon fire, of course. We had to purify the flames with spices, and a little dried salamander, though I was never quite sure that was necessary. Salamanders were terribly expensive, and they smell dreadful. Some of the stranger spell ingredients were only there to make money for the suppliers, I'm sure.'

'This way will work better,' the dragon told her, smoke spiralling smugly from his nostrils. 'Do go on.'

Lily caught her breath anxiously. She couldn't help worrying about this spell – whether it was gong to hurt her father somehow. Having an enchantment taken off you with dragon fire did sound quite risky.

'Well, in this case, since we're restoring something that's been taken...' Rose walked round Lily's father, staring at him thoughtfully, as if he was an interesting sort of project. 'I think I would suggest instilling your fire into the water, and having him drink it. Particularly as it's his voice he's lost. It seems appropriate. Do you think that would work?'

Daniel looked at her doubtfully. 'You can't put fire in water. I've tried all sorts of ways; it would be an excellent trick, really spectacular for the audience. But it's just too difficult. You can light oil floating on water, of course, but how's he going to drink that? We did have a fire swallower once, and believe me, he'd trained for a very long time. And he still wasn't all that good at it.'

Lily nodded. Drinking fire was just the sort of horrible thing she'd been worrying about.

'Magical fire. Mama taught me about that,' Georgie said quietly. 'You can put it into a liquid form. For – for bad things.' She shivered, turning a shade paler in the bright stage lights. Then she swallowed, and dug her nails into her palms as if she was swallowing the unruly spells back down inside her.

Lily swallowed too, forcing back her panic. They *would* heal Georgie, they had to. Lily would not give her up, and let her become some fearful weapon in their mother's hands.

'Unless dragon fire is different,' Georgie added, her voice small.

'Far better,' the dragon agreed. 'Are the words the same? *Unbind me, free me, loose me of my chains,* and so on?'

'Exactly. We could all say them together,' Rose suggested.

Lily glanced anxiously at her father, but he didn't seem worried by the thought of all this. In fact, he was nodding eagerly.

The dragon sighed, a little irritably. 'Lily, dear child. Take the bottle for me. Claws are not made for such things. Put it down in front of me. Between me and your father.'

Lily did as she was told, watching the silvery glow mist out of the bottle as she lifted it out of his talons. What would drinking that water every day do for the people in Fountain Court, she wondered, placing the bottle carefully on the stage. Maybe it was lucky – those children had looked like they could do with some luck. Lily smiled to herself. Perhaps she and Georgie had poured a little bit of magic into their lives.

The dragon shifted himself out further into the middle of the stage, and all the stagehands and theatre performers melted further back into the wings. There was a strong sense of magic about to happen, so strong that Lily was sure even those with no magic inside them could feel it. It was prickling across her skin, making her heart beat faster.

Argent twisted and rippled, stretching out his spine – and he was almost all spine – and mantling his wings. Then he hunched down low, his huge muzzle next to the bottle, as though he was going to swallow it. It wasn't even a mouthful.

Lily saw the jugglers who had been fighting huddle closer together, gripping each other's hands, and she felt Georgie and Henrietta press up against her. Georgie was shaking. Such a strong sense of magic all around must make it even harder for her to control the spells, Lily guessed. She caught her sister's hand, dry and feverish, and pressed it tightly.

The dragon's sides heaved, and then he let out a sudden sharp burst of flame, completely enclosing the stoneware bottle, which blackened and glowed red and then gold. And then it disappeared, leaving only the water, lapping and flame-shaped, shimmering above the wooden floor of the stage.

The dragon stepped back, and growled at Lily's father, as though the flames had scorched his throat. 'Drink it.'

How was he supposed to drink that, Lily wondered, feeling Georgie digging her nails into her palms, but her father seemed to know. He stumbled forward, sinking to his knees with the folds of the red dressing gown puddling around him, and then he scooped up the silvery flames in his hands.

Rose gestured to Lily and Georgie, holding out her hands, and began to chant in a low voice, 'Unbind me. Free me. Loose my chains.' She paused for a moment. 'Free my tongue. Release my voice. Let the magic pour through me once again.' Then she nodded to the girls, and they joined in, the three of them standing in a ring around Lily and Georgie's father. 'Unbind me... Free me... Loose my chains...'

Lily felt the words whisper through her, full of power, and she looked anxiously at Georgie. Would taking part in a spell like this waken the magic inside her? But her sister's face was white and set, and she was chanting fiercely, spitting each word out as though it hurt. She was determined to control the spells, Lily saw. She was fighting them.

'Unbind me,' Lily whispered. 'Free me...'

Her father held the water-flames dancing and licking around his hands, and lifted his cupped palms up to his mouth, pouring the silvery liquid down his throat and swallowing painfully in great tearing gulps. Then he dropped his hands, little silver dribbles running from between his fingers, and tipped slowly over onto his side, unconscious.

'What's happened?' Georgie cried, and she tore herself from the others and began to run towards him, but the dragon batted her aside with one massive claw.

'Wait...'

Lily caught Georgie and held her, and they clung together, watching as their father lay motionless on the stage for what seemed an age.

Then, very gradually, he began to move. Lily gasped as she saw his fingers clenching and fumbling at the wooden boards, as though he wasn't sure what they were. With slow, painful movements, he pulled himself up to his knees. Then he reached out his arms to Lily and Georgie, and as Lily ran to him, she saw that his eyes were clearer and wider than they'd been before, without that strange yellow cast of sickness.

Lily huddled against him, feeling his arm round her, and Georgie next to her. She didn't remember this – she knew it had happened before, it must have done, but she had no memory of her father before he was taken away. She could feel his magic now, so like her own, as it wrapped lovingly around her.

'My girls...' The voice was wavery, a little cracked from disuse, but it was there. 'My clever, brave girls...'

'It feels like a different country...' Peyton Powers sighed, frowning down at the newspaper spread out in front of him. He was still wearing the dressing gown, but now over a clean shirt and trousers borrowed from Daniel. They shouldn't really have fitted him, Lily thought, given that Daniel was only seventeen, and skinny, but feeding the prisoners hadn't been something the warders in Archgate prison cared a great deal about. It wasn't as if anyone particularly wanted them kept alive.

'Imagine how I felt,' Argent muttered, peering over his shoulder. His sight didn't adjust well to the fine print of newspapers and books, but he could puzzle out a few words here and there. 'When we hid ourselves away under Fell Hall, magic was flourishing, even though the Fell bloodline had failed. Then I wake up and discover that I'm illegal...'

Mr Powers, who seemed to have adapted remarkably well to living with a dragon, glanced up at him and snorted. 'I'm not convinced you ever were legal. I'll bet that Fell ancestor who first found himself a dragon never declared your people to the Crown. Any king with the first bit of sense would have had dragons as Crown property as fast as he could get the laws drawn up.'

'And you think that would have made any difference?' the dragon sniffed. 'I am not anyone's property, I thank you. We do not belong to the Fells. I do not *belong* to anyone. I merely – associate with the family.'

Henrietta sniffed loudly, and for once Gus seemed to agree with her, staring sceptically at the dragon, and muttering, 'For a few hundred years...'

'Are we related to the Fells?' Lily asked her father, hoping that this would distract the dragon. Henrietta was getting too familiar with him, Lily thought. She'd forgotten that she was perfectly mouthful-sized. 'Argent says we must be, and Rose thinks we probably are.'

Rose nodded. 'I should know, but I wasn't brought up at Fell Hall, so I missed out on a great deal of family history. Lily has a look of the family portraits, though, sometimes. As do you, Peyton.'

Mr Powers looked up from the newspaper, frowning a little. 'Your great-grandmother was a Fell, Lily. Did you not know?'

Argent gave a satisfied sigh. Dragons did not lower themselves to saying *I told you so*, but it was quite clear he meant it.

Lily's father shook his head. 'Of course you didn't... I keep forgetting that Nerissa taught you nothing – and I still think you were the lucky one.' He glanced towards the pile of dustsheets where Georgie was sleeping, great black shadows circling her eyes. She spent more and more time asleep now, saying that it was easier to control the spells that way. 'I hate to think of you both at Merrythought, with your mother and that strange servant of hers. And even now...' He frowned. 'That you should both grow up with your magic having to be kept secret like this. It's so wrong, I hate it. We should be proud...'

Lily swallowed. 'You sound like Mama. Except – she would be angrier.'

He sighed. 'I'm not suggesting we join the conspiracy, Lily, don't worry. But we must do *something*. I can't live without my magic. You don't understand. That binding they had on me, and the spells throughout the prison, they made it impossible for me to feel anything. I was just a husk, dried out and feeble. But now!' He smiled at her. 'I may look old and decrepit, Lily, but I feel full of power. The thought of hiding it for the rest of my life, pretending it doesn't exist. How could I?'

Lily nodded doubtfully. Magic had to be hidden – it was just the way it was. But she could see that her father didn't understand. 'If we show what we are, you'll be slung straight into prison again, and us with you,' she began slowly.

He was shaking his head already. 'No! No, don't you see, Lily, I don't think we will. Of course, if we're caught... But we won't be. We'll have to be very careful.'

'Careful doing what, exactly?' Henrietta demanded suspiciously, planting her front paws firmly on the newspaper and glaring at him. 'It took a great deal of effort to rescue Lily and her sister from that foul place, you know. I'm not having her taken away and shut up again.'

'Nor am I,' Peyton Powers said grimly. 'Nor am I, Henrietta, don't worry. But you're all in a prison even here, don't you see? Shut away from your own magic. It needn't be that way. There are hints, even in here.' He shook the newspaper. 'These crackdowns, our brave protectors fighting against lawlessness. It's the lawlessness I'm interested in, not how a brave officer was taken to hospital. People are standing up to the Queen's Men. So now's our chance!' He turned eagerly to Lily. 'Lily, flower, you said that the children liked the magic, by the fountain, didn't you?'

Lily swallowed, the pet name suddenly familiar. Did she really remember him calling her his little flower? Or did she only wish she remembered? 'Yes,' she thought to say at last. 'One of the boys said they should report us, but that was only because he thought they might be in trouble if they were found harbouring magicians, I think. The others were so pleased that we made the fountain run again, they only cared that it should stay. And it wasn't just for the drinking water that they liked it. It drew them close. They were almost warming themselves at it, like a fire.'

'Very few people actually think magic is wrong, it seems to me,' her father mused. 'Only the queen – and the Dowager, and their advisors. We would have the support of the everyday people, if we were to demand the Decree be repealed.'

Rose frowned. 'Not if magic – and magicians – were the same as they always were,' she said slowly. 'Expensive, and special, and the magicians always so proud and disdainful.'

'I was never –' Peyton Powers stopped, and

sighed. 'Well, perhaps I was. But now, my dear lady, I would happily work on the most everyday charms. I would cure warts, if it meant I could use my magic. I would invent a spell to stop black beetles in the larder. A little magic shop...'

'There was a wonderful shop, Sowerby's, do you remember?' Rose smiled. 'It had the most terrifying stuffed crocodile...'

Lily's father snorted with laughter. 'One of my apprentice friends hatched a plot to steal that crocodile. He was planning to set him free in the lake in St James's Park, to chase all the fashionable ladies out walking. He nearly lost an arm, and old Gideon Sowerby dug up a charm from somewhere – he wasn't a magician himself, of course, but he knew enough to use some of his stock – anyway, he flung a handful of this strange ointment at the poor boy, and he smelled of roses for the next year.'

'But that sounds nice,' Lily objected, and her father shook his head.

'Not at the strength Alastair was wearing it. You simply couldn't stay in the same room with him. It wore off, eventually, but even years afterwards, there was still a very slight scent...' He chuckled, remembering. 'But don't you think, ma'am, that life would be better, for everyone, with just a little magic in it?'

'Well, of course!' Rose snapped. 'Are you proposing to join this conspiracy, then, along with your wife?' She stared at him, her eyes burning coldly, like ice crystals.

'No!' Lily gasped, staring at her father in horror. 'You can't, even if we want the same thing! Not after what they've done to Georgie.'

Her father jumped up, snatching her by the shoulders and staring down at her. 'I would never, never stoop to that,' he said angrily, glancing between her and Rose. 'We don't want the same thing at all, Lily! But we can't let things go on like this. I want a peaceful rebellion, if such a thing could happen. I don't want to overthrow the queen – only to make her see that magic isn't the monster she's been persuaded it must be. Besides, Jonathan Dysart and your mother and the rest of them want to go back to the old ways, with the magicians lording it over everyone else. Rose is right. That isn't how it should be at all.'

Lily nodded. 'I don't think the Dowager Queen will ever let magic be legal again,' she told him sadly. 'Not when it was a magician who murdered the old king. I know she's mad, and hateful, but you can understand why. And she's in charge now, isn't she? She's even called the Queen Regent, now that Queen Sophia is so ill.'

Her father frowned, and squeezed her shoulders. 'I

know. But if we manage to expose the plot, then perhaps they'll believe us.' Then he let go of Lily and slumped back down against Argent with a defeated sigh. 'Except that telling the queen that there's been a widespread and carefully organised plot by a group of renegade magicians is hardly the way to get her to trust us, is it... Even more so when I'm married to one of them. It's all so tangled.'

'It is all you can do,' Argent said simply. 'Especially as your daughters are caught up in it already.'

'I know. You're right. The first thing is to help Georgie.' Mr Powers nodded, glancing at her anxiously. 'I hate to wake her. Taking part in the spell yesterday seems to have drained her completely. To see her like this makes my stomach turn – especially when I am so much improved... But the sooner we start to release her from her mother's magic the better.'

'Now?' Lily asked, her eyes hopeful.

Her father nodded. 'Now.'

FOUR

Lily shook her sister gently, and Georgie moaned in her sleep, her eyes fluttering under their bruised lids.

'Maybe we should let her sleep just a little longer,' her father suggested, staring down at her worriedly.

But Lily shook her head. 'I don't want her like this any longer than she has to be.' She shook Georgie a bit harder, and then patted her cheek, more firmly than she should have done. Georgie woke up, gasping, her eyes staring open in panic.

'What is it? What's happened?'

'Nothing...' Lily shushed her, as she did during the strange nightmares her sister woke with now, thrashing and whimpering in the old brass bed they shared. She was used to Georgie's frights, but their father winced at her terrified face.

Georgie leaned against Lily's shoulder, letting out a shaky sigh. 'I thought – I was dreaming...'

'I know. But it isn't the magic, Georgie.' She wrapped her arm close round her sister, squeezing her tight. 'We're safe, I promise. Georgie, listen – Father thinks we can start to work on the spells. Lifting them. You can be yourself again!' She held Georgie at arm's length, staring into her eyes. 'It's what we've been wanting all this time! Aren't you excited?' she asked, feeling oddly flat. She had expected Georgie to be delighted, laughing – smiling at least. But all her sister did was stare at her, with those big frightened eyes.

'She doesn't know what her own self is,' a small, gruff voice said, from by Lily's elbow.

Lily glanced down at Henrietta, frowning. 'Don't be silly.'

'She's right,' Georgie whispered. 'I really don't. I've had Mama's spells inside me for so long. Years and years.' She swallowed painfully. 'What if there isn't any of *me* left?'

Henrietta leaned forward, her eyes bulging earnestly, and Lily caught her breath. Usually, the black pug took every opportunity she could to snipe at her sister. She'd never been sure why. Henrietta was so perfect, and Lily adored her – bringing Henrietta out of that painting at Merrythought, as a real dog, had been her first ever spell. Or the first one that had worked, anyway. But she did wonder sometimes if Henrietta was jealous of Georgie. If that was why she snapped, and called her sister feeble. But she couldn't ever ask her.

Now she tried desperately to think at Henrietta, to warn her that this wasn't the time for one of her snide little comments about Georgie spending all her time in the theatre wardrobe, instead of doing anything useful. Calling Georgie wet wouldn't help at all right now. But the little dog only nudged her damp black nose against Georgie's wrist, and gazed up at her.

'I can smell you,' she told Georgie firmly. 'You're in there. Wrapped up in something dark, yes. But that's all it is. A dark blanket, sewn up around you.'

Lily shivered. It sounded too much like a shroud. But Georgie was smiling, just a little, and her cheeks were faintly pink.

'You're sure?' she whispered, and Henrietta reverted to her normal, snappish self.

'Of course I'm sure. What do you think I am, a cat?'

Gus's whiskers twitched slightly and he glanced up at Rose, but he pretended that he hadn't heard.

Henrietta flicked her tail triumphantly. 'So. How do we start?'

Mr Powers frowned, and held out his hand to Georgie, wrapping it around her thin fingers. He was trying to smile, but his arm brushed against Lily, and she could feel that he was shaking.

'Girls, you have to understand. Nerissa, your mother, is a very strong magician.'

Lily nodded, and swallowed. 'Stronger than you?'

'Maybe,' her father admitted.

But Rose was shaking her head.

'I don't believe that. Different, yes. And more ruthless. But your magic runs very deep, Peyton Powers. I saw it in you a long time ago, and I've seen it in Lily.' She smiled at Georgie's miserable face, and knelt down beside her. 'And the pug dog is right, however much she delights in tormenting Gus. I'm sure your father's magic is in you, Georgie, just as much as your mother's is. Nerissa's magic is so strong because she set no limits on it. Ever. I could feel angry spells seething through every inch of her when she came to see me. She is just as much under the control of her spells as you are. The difference is that she called them in. She welcomed them. They're part of her now. All of her, who knows? She'd be nothing without them. I don't believe the same is true of you. And as for you.'

She rounded on their father. 'Remember that you've just spent nine years in prison for your magic. If you didn't think much of it, why didn't you just give it up? You could have hidden away quietly with your beautiful daughters and protected them from *her*! Practised a few little spells on the side... Why did you abandon them, if your magic is such a feeble, worthless thing?'

Peyton Powers stared down at Georgie's hand, unconsciously stroking her fingers. 'I was strong once. But now – you don't understand how strange it feels. You set those spells in Archgate well, you know. They drained the magic out of me. Deadened it, so I could hardly feel it at all.' He laughed bitterly. 'I feel as though I'm an apprentice all over again. Learning how to use my magic after such a long time shut away from it. I don't know if I can fight Nerissa's spells well enough.' He swallowed. 'And I don't want to hurt you,' he added to Georgie.

'I don't care.' For the first time in weeks Lily saw a fire light in her sister's eyes, snapping and sparkling. 'Don't you think it hurts when I can feel the spells fighting inside me? I thought I could just bury the spells and it would be all right, but I can feel them turning me into someone else now. I'd rather die than stay like this!'

'No!' Lily yelped. 'You mustn't say that!'

'It's true,' Georgie whispered, the sparks dying as her eyes filled with tears.

Henrietta growled faintly and clambered into Georgie's lap, curling up in a determined fashion and laying her soft muzzle on Georgie's hand. Georgie stroked her cautiously, as though she wasn't sure it was allowed. Having the dog curled into her lap seemed to calm her, and Georgie swallowed.

'I don't care what you have to do to get the magic out of me. Just do it, whatever. Even if it takes all my own magic too. I hardly remember using it. I could only risk the tiniest spells anyway, before I'd feel something else coming to join them. Great big shadowy things, sliding along behind me, and then they'd slip into my shadow when I turned round. But I'd still know they were there, grinning at me. Now they don't even bother to hide. They're in charge, as soon as I even think about a spell. I wouldn't have risked the magic at the fountain if I hadn't been desperate. And then I collapsed before – before something awful happened. I'd much rather be just a girl, with no magic at all. I wouldn't even mind that very much.'

She smiled faintly at Lily and her father and Rose. 'If you could avoid me dying that would be nice... But I did mean it. This isn't me. Henrietta's right. I may not know what *me* is any more, but there must be something of me left.' She nodded determinedly. 'Even if there isn't a lot of me... I'd rather be real.'

Lily nodded miserably, and Henrietta licked Georgie's wrist and then nuzzled gently against her, rubbing her wrinkled little face up and down Georgie's arm. Georgie watched her in surprise – it was the sort of thing Henrietta did to Lily, never to her.

'Sit with me, dear one,' Argent suggested. 'All of you. I can protect you from the spells, a little, anyway. I am very curious about this magic of your mother's. I shall be interested to see it undone.'

Georgie nodded, and stood up carefully, still carrying Henrietta, although she kept looking at the dog anxiously, as though she expected to be snapped at to put her down. She settled between Argent's forelegs, with her father and Lily on either side, and Rose close by. Argent stretched his huge head out along one of his front legs, curling his neck around them so that they were almost enclosed in silver scales, and the strange sea-salt smell of dragon. Lily pressed her fingers against his scales, feeling the silky, china smoothness and the bumpy ridges where each scale joined the next. His magic buzzed and thrummed around her protectively, and she sighed, feeling a little of her fear lift away. He wouldn't let the spells hurt Georgie, she was sure of it. She pushed her other hand into Georgie's, and her sister gripped her fingers tightly. Then Henrietta laid her chin over their clasped hands, wrapping them in soft velvet-furred warmth.

Lily looked up at her father, wondering how he was going to start. His eyes were closed, and he was scowling, his dark, pointed eyebrows drawn together. He had already started searching for the spells, she realised, closing her eyes too, and trying to feel what he was doing. 'It *is* as though the spells are sewn into you,' he muttered. 'How odd. Nerissa never so much as stitched a sampler, I'm sure of it...'

'She's been living with this magic a long time,' Argent muttered slowly. 'Georgie has shaped it to fit herself.'

Georgie shook her head. 'I haven't... I don't want it. That sounds as though I made it part of me.' The dragon purred soothingly at her, and breathed out a faint, glittering mist. Lily watched it wreathe around her sister's shoulders and settle on her skin like a gleaming shield.

'It's so tight,' their father murmured. 'Woven into you. Georgie, can you feel this, if I pull...' His hand stirred, his fingers pinching together, as though he had found a thread, and Georgie giggled.

'It tickles.'

'It's like unravelling a piece of embroidery. So hard

to see...'

Rose laid her hand gently on his knee. 'Can you see it as a piece of embroidery? As a picture? Lily told us you made a picture on the wall. If your magic works in pictures, and Georgie's works with threads, then perhaps you can mix both together. My own old teacher used to knit her spells, sometimes. It might help for us all to lend you our strength, too. If we can see what's happening.'

'Yes,' Mr Powers whispered. 'I should have thought of it myself. So out of practice...' Lily saw him bite down hard on his lip, and then Georgie squeaked, and clutched at her stomach as though something had been pulled inside her. The dull grey cloth backdrop that masked the dragon when he wasn't to be seen by the audience unrolled and fell down from the flies about them in a shuddering rush.

Lily heard an angry shout from one of the stagehands, quickly silenced as they realised what was happening. It was like watching a picture being painted onto the dark cloth. A picture made of millions of delicate, intricately knotted stitches. A tapestry, Lily supposed. There had been some old, faded hangings in the hallway at Merrythought, but they were so damaged by years of sunlight that only the ghosts of the designs had been left. This tapestry was alive, and jewel-bright.

The stitches danced and glittered, pulsing with magic.

'Is that what I look like inside?' Georgie whispered, her eyes wide. She reached out her hand, wanting to stand and stroke the bright stitches, and her father gently pulled her back.

'I don't think you can touch it – it isn't really there. It's only a picture – an imagining, built out of both of our magics.'

'Do we have to unpick all of it?' Lily murmured. It was enormous, and so complicated – hundreds and hundreds of interwoven pictures that moved as she tried to stare at them, as if they were sliding away from her eyes. If she looked hard enough at one part of the pattern, and tried to think of it as only sewing, and not part of her sister, then she could see the stitches, but it made her eyes burn, and water.

'No,' her father muttered. 'There are darker threads, do you see? It takes a little while to pick them out. In a lot of the small images, it's as though they're sewn with a double thread.'

'Two strands of silk on the same needle,' Rose agreed. 'A trick, to mix your colours. It adds depth to the embroidery.'

'Well, it's done that here... Sewn in and out of your life story, Georgie. This thread of dark magic...' Her father sighed.

'Not all of it,' Lily said suddenly, rubbing her hand across her watering eyes and staring up at the central part of the picture hanging above them. 'Look, in the middle. It's brighter there. As though it's been sewn without the shadow thread.'

Her father nodded. 'The magic doesn't go all the way through you,' he told Georgie, squeezing her hand. 'But you can see how tightly it's sewn in. How much we need to unpick.'

'What happens if we can't?' Lily asked in a small voice, but no one answered. In so many of the tiny pictures, the darker thread was part of the design, greying out the brightness of her sister almost entirely. She strained her eyes to stare at one of the darkest, and shivered, seeing that eerie dust-wolf that Georgie had called up to save them from Mama's servant, Marten. She'd had to use one of the strange, dark spells inside her, and Lily remembered how horribly strong it had been, and how easily the black spell had flowed from Georgie's fingers, building their guardian out of street dust, and a little blood from the scratches Marten's claws had made. And then how quickly it had turned on them, after Marten had been despatched. It was hungry, and only Lily's weather magic had defeated it. It was magic she hardly knew she had, the calling of storms, something the Powers children had always been known for. She had felt it inside, when Henrietta had reminded her of her own growing magic.

The stitched wolf had a dusty grey coat with a dark reddish tinge, and Marten was backing away from it, greenish spell-flesh torn and leaking as she tried to flee back to their mother. If they pulled out all the dark threads here, then there'd be hardly any picture left, just Lily, clinging in panic to Henrietta, and the storm cloud gathering above waiting to wash the dust-wolf away into the gutters.

'It isn't just a dark thread,' Lily said, frowning. 'I mean, Henrietta's black, and she's in the tapestry – it's a different sort of darkness. There's an intensity to it. It sucks the colours out.' She tried not to glance at Georgie as she heard herself say it, but she didn't need to see her to remember her sister's white-fair hair and the grey paleness of her skin.

'Where does it start?' their father murmured, stretching out a hand towards the tapestry, as he tried to trace the dark thread back. Everyone stared at the stitching, daunted by the shadows woven through it, until Georgie stood up, with Henrietta in her arms, and pointed. Argent curled his tail away, so that they could walk towards the tapestry, but his wings were hunched forward, as though he wanted to shelter them all in his magic.

'Here.' Georgie's voice was very flat, and Lily could tell that she was squashing her feelings down, in case she cried. Or screamed, perhaps. She stood up too, and went closer, looking where Georgie pointed. Their father did something with the magic, and the curtain swayed in a breeze that wasn't there, and that part of the tapestry shifted and grew larger. Lily shivered as she looked at the embroidered version of her sister, so much younger, her cheeks fatter and pinkened, but already so serious-looking. Lily was sure she couldn't be more than seven. She was standing with their mother, and Lily recognised the library at Merrythought House, the dark wood of the furniture, and here and there the clever glint of gold thread, showing the gilded lettering on the leather of the books. Nerissa Powers had Georgie's hands in hers, and her little daughter stood in front of her, her arms lifted up. Their mouths were open, as they chanted a spell together, and their mother was smiling. A dark thread was coiling out of her mouth and wreathing itself around Georgie, blurring the brightness of her fair hair and smudging her pink dress with shadows.

'It started there,' Georgie said, in a small, shaken voice. Lily hissed and clawed at the picture with her nails, suddenly furious and desperate to rip it out. The threads caught in her nails and stuck to her fingers, sticky and burning. But that first dark thread was hanging loose now, trailing out of the design, flapping a little, like a pinned snake.

'Lily, be careful!' her father shouted, catching her hands as they went to rip at it again. 'Look at Georgie!' Lily did – and frowned. There were holes in the picture now, where she'd ripped the stitching out, but then, that was what they wanted, wasn't it? The child in the picture was smiling, still, even if she was a bit patchy.

'Look at her!'

Then Georgie moaned and Lily realised what he meant. The real Georgie, the one who was lying on the floor, her arms wrapped tightly round her chest, while Henrietta scratched frantically at her head.

'Pulling the thread out did that?' Lily whispered, horrified. Georgie moaned again, and twisted, and then her eyes opened, their blue darkened with tears.

'Keep going! If I can feel it like this, it must be working. You were wrenching something out of me, but it felt right, Lily, in an awful sort of way.'

'I'm not sure I can,' Lily faltered, watching Georgie writhe as the spells convulsed inside her again.

'Hurry!' Georgie wailed, and Lily turned resolutely away from her sister. With her teeth gritted, she hooked her nails into the next scene, one she almost remembered. Georgie was sitting in the library, a stack of books piled around her, her long hair trailing across the page as she studied the huge book in front of her. The book itself was spewing out shadowy magic this time, and Georgie was swallowed up inside it, reaching herself into the darkness and letting it suck her in.

I wonder where I was? Lily thought to herself. Perhaps out on the beach, or running through the overgrown orchards with Peter, happily forgotten. *I was so lucky.* Closing her eyes for a moment – but wishing she could close her ears too – Lily tore at the threads, ripping and pulling, shredding the book and its strangling magic, and leaving her sister sitting reading nothing. It wasn't until the shadowy coils of the book were gone, though, that Lily saw the figure by the window, turning back to look at her daughter. Her *daughters*, maybe. Lily had a strange feeling that even through the clever spell that turned all this into so much thread, her mother could see what she was doing. So much so that when a thin, high scream made her pull her clawed fingers away, for a moment she thought her mother was howling at her from inside the spell.

But it was Georgie, whiter than ever, her eyes black and open but seeing nothing as she screamed and banged her hands against the floor.

'Lily, stop it! It's too much for her.' Rose lifted Georgie's head onto her lap and began to croon to her in sweet spells of healing and comfort. 'The silks are binding you back together, sweetness. Darning the holes,' she murmured. 'Feel yourself knitting back together, growing strong and whole... *Stitch her, bind her, heal her, stitch her...*' she repeated, weaving her fingers over Georgie's heart.

Lily started to cry, hating herself for hurting her sister so, but Henrietta barked sharply at her to be picked up, and she clung to the little dog, gulping back tears.

'She asked you to. And it needs doing.'

'Yes, but look at her...' Lily moaned. 'What if she *dies*?'

Her father turned from helping Rose, and beckoned Lily over. 'Remember what she said. She was certain it would be better that way.'

'Then you think she is going to...' Lily sobbed.

He shook his head. 'No. But I don't think she's cured, either. Sorry, Lily. This went on too long. Years and years. Layers and layers of spells. It's going to take more than just one try. We have to do this slowly if we want anything of her to be left when we're finished.' He swallowed. 'I have seen people who've had spells torn out of them, Lily. If you're not careful, you can take everything else too, and then they're just a husk.'

'I can hear you, you know,' a tiny voice said from the floor. 'And I still don't care. Keep trying.'

Lily crouched down beside her. 'Tomorrow, if you're well enough, yes? You'll cast the spell again, won't you?' she added to her father. 'To make the tapestry.' Lily smiled down at her sister, trying to look as though she didn't feel torn too. 'Tomorrow, please can I use your good sewing scissors? Look, I've torn one of my nails nearly off on your stupid spell!'

She didn't look the same. Last time Lily had seen their mother properly, she had been in disguise, under a glamour that turned her into a crotchety old lady, on board the ship taking them to New York. Now she was back to her old self, wearing one of the stiff silk dresses Lily remembered so well, sweeping along the dusty floors at Merrythought, with one of her cats padding after her. Why didn't she have a familiar, Lily wondered, with sleepy dream-logic, and her mother smiled, baring too many teeth. *Why would I want a cat to tell me what to do, little Lily flower? I prefer my pets silent, or bound to me with a little more than loyalty.*

Lily nodded slowly, remembering the spell-creatures. Marten, her mother's spell-flesh servant, and the foul parrot that she had used to complete her old-lady disguise.

Now, why am I in your dream, little flower, and not with my Georgiana?

I don't know, Lily murmured. She was too asleep to be frightened, but she was conscious of a faint sense of worry. That this was not a good thing that was happening. That she *ought* to be scared.

The spells should lead me straight to Georgiana, her mother went on, sweeping further along the passageway of the dream, and then swirling round, her stiff skirts rustling, the orange-red silk glowing like flames in the dark. *Unless of course someone has been tampering with them,* she said, striding out of the darkness towards Lily, her dark eyes glittering with anger. *Have you, Lily? Have you been touching things you shouldn't? I can feel it – and there are broken spells staining your fingers. That was really very stupid, Lily. And very clever, all at the same time. Clever, and stupid, and surprising. You should not be able to break a spell of mine, not by yourself. So who has been helping you, that's the question. Georgiana would not be able to break the spells herself... Who have you found?* Her eyes widened, and the shine died out of them as she leaned over the bed, so that they looked like dull black stones. 'Surely not...' she murmured, reaching out a pale hand, her fingers impossibly long. They were almost touching Lily now, closer and closer – until Lily screamed, and hit her hand away, and woke up.

FIVE

'What is it?' Lily felt arms close around her, and for a moment she fought them, but then she realised she was awake, and this was Georgie. 'It's me, Lily, stop it, what's the matter? Did you have a bad dream?'

Lily nodded slowly, blinking in the darkness of their room at the theatre. She could feel Georgie beside her, and Henrietta on her knees. The black dog was staring at her anxiously, eyes glowing faintly greenish, like little lamps. 'You don't dream often,' she growled. 'Not like that.'

'I know,' Lily muttered, her voice dry and husky. 'Did you see?'

'Only flashes. Of her. That's who it was, yes? Your mother?'

'Mama?' Georgie's arms went suddenly tighter around her, and Lily clung back just as hard. The pair of them were knotted together, wrapped around each other like vines.

'It was just a dream,' Lily whispered hopefully.

'Really?' Georgie sighed. 'Have you ever dreamed of her before?'

Lily shook her head.

'So why now? I don't think it was a dream. It was a prophecy, maybe a foretelling.'

'No. It was happening right then. She was there. I think she saw me, and she knew what I'd done. She said I'd been meddling with her spells.' Lily swallowed. 'I think she might be coming to stop us.'

'She doesn't know where we are,' Henrietta put in quickly, but Lily was silent. 'Does she?'

'We tampered with the spells,' Lily whispered. 'I don't know how they work. Maybe she can follow them, if they're calling to her. Maybe she can find us.'

'She never could before,' Georgie said doubtfully. 'That's why she had to send Marten, to sniff us out, when we first ran away.'

'But remember how the spells started to come alive, when she got close to you in New York?' Lily reminded her. She was getting used to the darkness now. Georgie's face was a pale blur, with a glint of worried eyes.

'They've grown stronger, and she's linked to them, somehow.' She could feel Georgie's ribs heaving with her quick, panicked breaths. She laid her cheek gently against her sister's shoulder. 'Mama doesn't know we have Argent, remember. And she doesn't have any Fell blood in her like we do. She won't understand him like us, and he won't want to help her. He's on our side.' Lily was almost sure he was, anyway. She had a sense that dragons could be unpredictable.

Georgie stroked her hair. 'I suppose that is quite a big advantage,' she agreed, laughing a little.

Lily giggled in the darkness, 'Quite big, yes,' and Georgie elbowed her.

When they woke again, they could hear the usual bustle of the theatre around them, and Lily realised they had slept late. 'We should go and tell Father, I suppose,' she said to Georgie, as they dressed, buttoning each other up hurriedly, and splashing their faces from the jug and bowl of water they kept on a stool in the corner.

When they went up to the stage, they found their father with Daniel and Peter, discussing possible new tricks, while Argent slept stretched out along the back of the stage, as if he really were a piece of scenery. Scene painters were pottering around him, even climbing over him here and there, as they painted a new set of flats for one of the ballet acts.

Daniel was showing their father the pistol for the bullet catch and he was admiring the sugar-coated bullets, hefting them in his hand and comparing their weight to the real ones.

'Oh no, not that again,' Lily muttered. 'I told you how they nearly killed someone, didn't I?' she reminded Georgie.

'Hello!' Daniel waved to them excitedly. 'Your father has come up with some very interesting suggestions for the illusion, to make it seem more real. Apparently, one can make a most convincing fake blood, just from a certain kind of dried beetle!'

Lily nodded. 'Where's Rose?' she asked.

'Gone to see if she can find an old friend,' her father explained. 'She wants to get hold of some spell ingredients, to protect Georgie when we try to unravel the thread magic again. This friend of hers runs a – ummm – black market operation, finding that sort of thing for people like us...'

Lily nodded. That was a perfectly sensible thing for Rose to do. The right thing to do, in fact. If there weren't a ruthless, half-mad magician searching out the very child you were trying to protect. They needed Rose to be here, right now, helping them cast some kind of warding spells around the theatre, perhaps.

Peter was staring at her curiously. He twitched his eyebrows at her in a way that would usually make her want to laugh.

'What's the matter, little flower?' her father asked, seeing her and Peter exchanging glances.

Lily looked at him silently for a moment. She really didn't know how to tell him. After all, Nerissa Powers was their mother, but she'd been his wife first. Had he missed her, when he'd been in prison? He hated that she was involved in the plot to overthrow the queen, but Lily didn't know what else he felt about her.

'Your wife's coming,' Henrietta told him bluntly.

'Nerissa? Here?'

'I dreamed her here. I'm really sorry,' Lily whispered.

'No, it isn't your fault. We should have thought, of course, that the spells would bring her.' He sat down wearily on the edge of one of the cabinets, and Lily watched Daniel flinch. It wasn't a good idea to sit on them. You never knew quite what hidden mechanism might pop out. But her father seemed not to have set off anything dangerous. 'We should ward the theatre,' he muttered, gazing around and starting to count doors. But Lily wasn't listening any more.

The pinkness that had come back to Georgie's cheeks after their work yesterday, just the faintest flush of colour, had drained away again. She was twitching, her fingers clenching and unclenching, her eyes darting from side to side.

'Now? Already?' Lily gasped.

'She's coming!' Georgie hissed.

It wasn't an answer to Lily's question. The spells wouldn't let Georgie hear. A faint, pinkish vapour had started to issue from her nose and mouth, like Argent's magical smoke. Perhaps that was where she'd learned it, or the magic inside her had. Lily took a step closer, and the mist swirled into her hair, coating it with some sort of cold sticky substance. She had no idea what it was – and she was pretty sure Georgie hadn't either.

As the pinkish film coated her mouth and nose and eyes, Lily blinked, feeling her blood begin to slow down and cool inside her. Her thoughts slowed too, congealing into a dull acceptance of whatever it was she must do.

Peter caught up the polishing rag he used on the cabinets, and smothered the stuff in it, scrubbing it away from Lily's face and throwing the rag onto the wooden boards in disgust, watching it blacken and sizzle.

'Are you all right? It was some sort of control spell,' her father muttered, turning away from his half-started warding, and looking at the charred fabric with horror.

'To make you do whatever Nerissa wanted.' He nudged the ashes with his foot. 'This was Georgie's own blood she used, I think.'

'The colour out of her cheeks,' Lily agreed miserably. 'She was looking better than she had in ages, since we'd started loosening the spells. This magic's going to kill her. Georgie! Georgie! Can't you stop?'

Georgie's eyes seemed to snap into focus for just a second, and they were pleading with Lily. *Help me!* It was her sister's voice in her head, frightened and desperate.

She'll make me hurt you, I can't stop her!

Lily nodded. She caught her sister's hands, flinching a little at their cold deadness. It was as though the spells didn't really need Georgie's body at all, it was just a shell for the essence of her sister, deep inside. They drew all the life and warmth of her far down into themselves. That was what Lily had to protect, from the spells, and their mother. But if Georgie slept, unconscious, then surely the spells would be trapped inside her. It had happened before, when the spells first began to take her over – she would force herself to faint, so that she couldn't be made to hurt anyone. It was what she had done by the fountain.

'Lie down,' Lily told her, thinking it as hard as she could as well as saying it. Her sister's eyes rolled back, showing eerie whites, and then Georgie collapsed. Lily half caught her as she crumpled to the floor in her eagerness to be gone, and then Peter was there, helping her lower Georgie down. Lily rubbed her fingertips together over Georgie's eyelids, imagining sleep dust dropping into her sister's eyes and sparkling over the purplish lids, sealing her away from the magic. Georgie wriggled, and then seemed to smile for a moment, and then the life in her died away, leaving her just a huddled little mass of clothes.

'Nerissa.'

Lily wasn't used to all the nuances of her father's voice yet, but the darkness of his tone still shocked her. She turned slowly round, and saw her mother standing in the aisle that ran down the middle of the theatre. She was wearing the rust-red dress that she'd had on in Lily's dream, and she was smiling again too.

'I've been looking for you, Lily,' she said, her voice far sweeter than Lily ever remembered it being. 'For a very long time.'

'You mean Georgie,' Lily stuttered, her voice breaking and squeaking from fear. Had their mother even forgotten which of them was which?

'Mmmm...' Her murmur was like honey, dripping into Lily's ears and mouth. Mama had never bothered to use charm on her before. She had never *noticed* her before. 'Yes. Georgiana at first. And of course I could follow Georgiana through the spells, once you helpfully decided to wake them properly for me. But now I think I should have paid more attention to you when I had you, Lily. Perhaps I chose the wrong daughter.'

Lily had daydreamed about her mother saying this for years. She had wished that *she* was the special one, who had all Mama's attention. It was only later that she realised how lucky she had been, growing up unnoticed and unspoilt. Unshaped.

'You're not having either of them now, Nerissa.' Lily's father was standing behind her, his hands resting on her shoulders, and all at once her mother's honeyed voice seemed sickly, and her affection was so obviously false that Lily felt stupid, and ashamed of the way her heart had quickened.

'She's very good, isn't she?' Henrietta muttered, sitting down heavily on Lily's foot. 'Even I almost liked her for a moment there. Don't worry, Lily, I shall bite you if I think you're falling under her spell.'

'You left the girls in my care, Peyton dearest,' her mother purred, 'while you went off to be a hero, and made yourself completely useless.'

'And you decided to forget about me, and everything we promised each other, and join a gang of dangerous conspirators,' he spat back.

She shrugged. 'Conspirators who are going to bring our world back to the way it should be. To overthrow a tyrannical government, and restore us to our former glory.'

'Our former glory meant living a life of ease and luxury while we were oppressing most of our people,' he yelled angrily, and Nerissa laughed.

'Our people? Our people are the magicians, Peyton, and they all agree with me.'

'I don't!' Lily was brave enough to gasp.

Her mother walked closer to the stage, and Lily heard the silk of her dress hissing over the carpet. 'But you will, darling, don't worry.'

'I won't! I never will!' Lily said shakily. 'I know Queen Sophia is doing things badly, but we can't kill her. It's just not right...'

She could feel the warmth of her father's hands, resting on her shoulders, and his magic flowing into her, hesitant but loving. She sensed roots, growing down into the ground and drawing strong magic out of it, sending it out in branches over her head and sheltering her. It was so different from her mother's charms – her father was lending her his strength, even though he had so little of it, and it was there for her to use as she wished, not to force her into anything.

'Don't expect your father to protect you, Lily. He

really can't, not against me. He never could stand up to me.'

'What do you want with her?' Lily's father shouted. 'You've already made Georgie into your puppet, and now you want Lily too? I won't let you do this to them. I can't stop your crazed plotting, but I won't let you trap the girls in this madness.'

His wife stared back at him coolly. 'Darling, you can have Georgiana back. With pleasure. What's left of her. I want this one. She's my daughter, far more than she's yours. Where do you think she gets all her spirit from? And her strength? It isn't from you.'

Lily felt Argent shiver behind her, just a twitch in the magic that she was so used to now. He was awake, she realised, and listening. Waiting to see what would happen. And he disagreed, she thought. She could hear the discordant notes as he growled inside her head, huge and furious. Her power did come from her father, from the Fell blood he'd passed on to her, not her mother at all. It was a fabulous relief. The tightness of fear in Lily's chest eased a little, and she watched as her mother stepped closer again, her dark hair crackling as the magic whirled around her. She seemed taller, and infinitely more frightening.

We have something she doesn't, Lily told herself. *We have a dragon, and I have Georgie, and Peter, and Daniel and Father and Nicholas and Mary and everyone in the theatre. They love me for me, not because I could hurt them...*

But remember that you could, Lily, Argent hummed inside her head. *You do not understand yet, what you are able to do. Don't stop yourself. I am here, and I will help if I can, but I am not sure you need me as much as you think you do.*

'I shall take the spells from Georgiana – she was too weak, just like the others. I should have known. I hoped – such a waste of time, all three of them. But this one...' Nerissa Powers purred as she looked at Lily. 'This is the child I should have borne to start with. My true daughter.'

'I'm not!' Lily yelled, suddenly too angry to be frightened. 'I'm nothing like you!'

But her mother was advancing up the steps to the stage, and her father, Peter, Daniel and even Argent seemed frozen and powerless to stop her.

'You can't just take the spells out of Georgie,' Lily told her, her voice shaking. 'We tried, you know we did, that's how you found us. It hurt her too much. She would have died if we had kept going. We have to do it bit by bit.'

'Of course. Because she's so terribly weak.' Her mama smiled. 'But you aren't, Lily darling. And I am really very short of time.'

'She wants to put the spells into you...' Henrietta growled, pressing against Lily's legs. 'Get back, Lily, get away from her. I'll stop her. You run!'

'But she'll kill Georgie if she rips them out. She can't do that, not her daughter.' Lily shook her head, not able to believe that her mother would do such a thing.

'Of course she would, she did it to the others, didn't she? And if it goes wrong, putting the spells in will kill you too. Which isn't to say that would be worse than what she's planning anyway.' Henrietta snapped her teeth sharply. 'Run, Lily!'

Nerissa Powers laughed, an icy, grating sort of sound that she hadn't bothered to make pretty. 'I really wouldn't, darling. You won't get anywhere. Even with the dear little dog to protect you. Besides, you needn't be afraid. I'm practically sure you're strong enough to survive the transfer of the spells.' She smiled, stretching her lips out across her teeth. 'And if you aren't, at least I will have tried. There are the others, of course, but I so wanted one of the spell-children to be mine. My daughter could be so much stronger than those smug Dysart girls... It should be our family who are the ones to bring it all back, and restore us to our glory.' Her eyes glittered with excitement, and then suddenly dulled. 'But there's so little time left, only a few days. It has to work now!'

She turned abruptly away from Lily, and stooped over Georgie, stretching out her hands, as though to scoop up a handful of threads and tear them away.

'No!' Lily's father roared, pushing Lily aside and striding towards her. But his wife only smiled, and put one hand up to stop him.

'You won't. I know you won't.' Her voice swirled around him like a line of music, rising and falling, and Lily could see all at once from his face why he had loved her. Why he still did, for he stopped, his hands raised to hurl his wife away from his daughter. He was trying to take that last step forward, Lily could tell, but he couldn't quite bring himself to do it. In case he hurt her.

But when their mother reached down, and wound her hand in Georgie's hair to haul her up, as if she were nothing more than a doll, nothing she cared about, he flung himself at her at last.

He had delayed too long. He had been afraid to hurt Nerissa, but she didn't care about hurting him. The surge of magic she threw at him so carelessly was strong enough to burn Lily's eyes, leaving them spotted and flashing like the fireworks show over the river that Daniel had taken them to see.

He gasped and crumpled, and Nerissa turned away, not even waiting to see him fall. She stooped over Georgie once again, and when Lily raced to drag her sister away, her mama simply caught her, encircling her wrist in one iron hand. Lily kicked at her, and pulled, and even tried to bite her, but it was as if her mother simply didn't notice. She wrapped Lily in her arm, dragging her close, pushing her face down towards Georgie's, as if Georgie was to breathe the spells into her sister. Lily had an awful feeling that it might be her sister's last breath of all.

'No!' She wrenched at her mother's arm, turning her face away, and Henrietta darted in, sinking her teeth into the collar of Georgie's dress and trying to haul her back across the stage. But she was such a small dog, and Georgie, even when she was thin and pale and sick, was just too heavy.

It was the way she ignored them that was so awful, Lily thought, as the fear set in and time seemed to run into a strange, dreamy slowness. Their mother couldn't care less that Georgie looked half dead, and Lily was screaming, and her children's father lay bleeding on the floor. All she cared about were the spells. And now she was going to do it. Lily could see no one could stop her. Argent was trying to help, but he was simply too big to dive into the fight without hurting Lily and

Georgie too. He'd given up his scenery disguise now, and he was craning his neck close, hissing like an enormous snake, darting his head in and out but unable to strike.

Nicholas had raced out of the wings, and Lily thought he was trying to cast some sort of spell, but he was white-faced with panic and he could only make his fingers burn with greasy sparks. Daniel and Peter were standing behind him, watching in horror, but they had no magic – her mother could just squash them like flies.

If only Rose hadn't gone, Lily thought, letting out a long, moaning wail, as her mother's fingers forced her mouth open, and pulled on Georgie's hair to tip up her face. No one could do anything – she was still burning from the spell that had struck down her father, but now she could feel the still coldness of the magic her mother was summoning up to drag the spells out of Georgie. It was so strong. There was no way that Georgie could live through it, Lily thought dully. It would wrench everything out of her, she would be dust and bones.

There was nothing Lily could do. There was nothing anyone could do. The spells would take her over, and if there was anything of her left at all, it would be buried deep inside. A velvety, gentle darkness seemed to rise up behind Lily's eyes as she gave in. It was no use fighting.

Then something wrenched her back. Lily couldn't tell what the noise was at first. It came in distinct parts – a strange, tearing bang and then a slow whistle, and Lily felt her mother's grip loosen. She slid to the floor and wriggled painfully away, looking up and trying to see what had happened.

Peter was standing in front of their mother, both hands wrapped round the pistol from the bullet-catch trick. So Lily had been wrong – he might not have any magic, but it didn't make him helpless.

Had he actually shot their mother? She had been protected against spells, but perhaps not a bullet...

Nerissa had dropped Georgie again, and she was cradling her arm. Lily could see dark blood staining the sleeve of her dress, but it was only a flesh wound, nothing that would stop her for long.

Peter stared back at her defiantly. He had only had one bullet in the gun, and now it was gone, and all he could do was glare.

Lily screamed as she saw her mother raise her hands, and caught the glittering fury in her eyes. Lily wasn't sure if she recognised Peter as the mute servant boy who had lived at Merrythought for years. She wouldn't have cared anyway. He was just an annoyance, a little fly, to be batted out of her way. Another searing blast of power hurled him over the side of the stage, and Lily, sobbing, watched him fall.

'Nerissa Powers!'

Lily turned, and tried to run, and felt her mother's magic settle over her like a fiery net, holding her down against the stage. But inside, her own magic leaped up in delight as Rose marched out of the wings in her neat grey cloak, with Gus padding delicately behind her. Surely Rose was strong enough to fight their mother?

From the corner of her eye, Lily saw Daniel creep forward, and huddle Georgie into his arms, pulling her away towards Argent, who was coiling and twisting up and down the stage, and hissing steam and smoke like an angry teakettle. He tucked Georgie affectionately up in one foreleg and hustled Daniel behind him, out of the way.

Remember how strong you are, Lily! he told her silently. *Fight back! If I can join in without fear of hurting you more than I help, then I will!*

Lily tried, but the net burned her as she wriggled, a strange icy burning that seemed to leave dark scorches across the magic inside her. She couldn't move without it stinging her, and if she tried to summon her magic it seared across her skin, leaving her dizzy and sick.

'You don't deserve these children,' Rose snarled,

reaching down to pull Lily into her arms.

But Nerissa only laughed. 'I'm only trying to make a better world for them to live in,' she parroted, in a sweet singsong.

Even she didn't believe it, Lily realised. She wasn't really fighting for a world full of magic. It was all just an excuse. She enjoyed using her spells like this, that was all. She loved the chaos and fear she brought. She would be able to rule a whole country, Lily thought, shivering. That was what her mother wanted – nothing more or less than power.

Rose flinched as the net burned into her fingers, and in that moment of distraction, Lily's mother struck, sending her power surging into the net spell, so that it was suddenly so strong everyone could see it, stretched over Lily like a fiery web. It coiled and bit into Rose's hands, pulling her magic out of her to strengthen the spell even more, and she gasped. The more the old magician struggled, the more of her power it drained out. Gus wound himself around her ankles, mewing frantically as Rose collapsed to her knees with Lily clutching at her, trying to hold her up.

Nerissa watched, smiling. 'Poor Lily. Did you think she was going to save you? This old woman?' Then she frowned. 'What?'

For Lily's eyes had widened, staring out beyond her

mother to the back of the stage. Argent was rearing upright onto his hind legs, stretching out his enormous wings over his head so that they filled the whole space of the stage. He swooped the silvery folds around so that all of them were wrapped in a glittering cocoon.

Without realising, Lily's mother had pushed away all that had been protecting her. By pinning Lily and Rose down to the ground, she had left herself exposed, and the dragon could strike without fear of hurting his friends.

She screamed as she saw him coming, his incredible speed born of pure magic and desperate anger. Argent had watched her hurt Lily, and her father, and Rose, who were all linked to him by their Fell blood, and now he could take his revenge. He darted towards her, his claws scraping great gouges in the boards, and snapped her up in his massive jaws, like a cat snatching a mouse, dangling the tiny creature up in the air.

Noooo! It was a roar of furious, fiery magic. *You shall not!*

Lily could feel how angry he was, and she could sense what he was about to do. This woman had hurt his children, and he wanted to bite and dash and rend and claw. He wanted her dead.

But Lily didn't.

SIX

on't! Don't tear her up!' Lily gasped. 'We can't. If we do that, it means we're murderers.'

'She was trying to kill you!' Henrietta snarled back. 'Well, she might have killed you, if the spells had been too strong. And she definitely would have killed Georgie.' She looked across at Lily's father, slumped on the stage. 'She may have killed your father,' she added quietly. 'I can't even see Peter.'

'I know...' Lily gulped. 'But I don't want to be like she is.'

Argent shook the limp bundle in his jaws, and growled. 'You are far too gentle. She would have no hesitation in killing you. Your father held back, Lily, and she's half killed him.'

'Only half?' Lily asked, her voice wavering.

'He's alive,' the dragon admitted, almost reluctantly. He wanted to rip their mother apart, Lily could tell. She was making it harder for him. 'And so is Rose – but only just. Both of them will be weakened, for a long time.'

'Where's Peter?' Daniel asked, walking towards them, cradling the pistol in his hands. 'I saw him fall...'

Lily closed her eyes. She had been trying not to see that slow, flailing fall again, but it kept flashing in front of her. It reminded her horribly of the time Peter slid from Argent's back, and she'd thought he was lost. Now, she knew that he must be. The blast of her mother's magic had felled two great magicians. What chance did a poor mute servant child have?

'Over the front of the stage, between the gas lights,' she whispered. And then she looked up at Argent, and her voice shook as she told him bitterly, 'I take it back. You can eat her. I don't care.'

Henrietta looked up at her, her glittering black eyes sunken in the furry folds around her face. She liked Peter, Lily knew. She liked his quietness, his slow, methodical way of doing things. He could almost understand her, now, even though like Argent she didn't talk the same way a human would. She walked slowly, heavily over towards the edge of the stage, and looked out across the dark, dusty velvet of the seats. 'I can't see him,' she muttered, peering down reluctantly.

'You mean there's nothing *left*?' Lily's voice shook, and she laid Rose gently down and hurried to follow Henrietta, peering anxiously out into the auditorium. There was such a sense of breathless waiting that she could imagine the seats were all full. But this wasn't a trick. Daniel wasn't going to reveal that his young assistant was behind the velvet curtain after all, or miraculously back in one piece, or shooting up from a hidden trap door.

Or posing dramatically at the back of the auditorium. Lily swallowed, gazing at the figure in the darkness. Someone was there, standing at the back row of seats, and looking about as if he wasn't sure what was going on. Lily stared, as whoever it was walked shakily down the threadbare carpet. And then she jumped, shrieking, from the front of the stage, and flung herself stumbling at Peter.

'We thought you were dead! We thought she'd turned you into dust! How did you do it?'

Peter only shrugged wearily. He was very pale, but he seemed to be all in one piece as Lily pulled him back towards the stage.

'The spells, remember?' Henrietta nudged her cold nose into Lily's hand, and stood there looking down on them, her tail twisting importantly. 'All those spells from Fell Hall. He's immune now – the dragon said so, when he walked through your father's go-away spell.'

'I had forgotten,' Argent agreed, sounding surprised, and rather muffled, as he still had a mouthful of unconscious enchantress. He shook her a little, enjoying the way she swung limply in his jaws, and Lily shuddered. If they didn't work out what to do with her soon, he would eat her, Lily was sure.

'Please don't do that again,' she told Peter, as he gave her a leg up onto the stage, and she hauled him after her. 'You always seem to end up saving us. It isn't that I'm complaining, but if you keep doing it you'll get hurt. Did you know she couldn't get you with a spell?'

Peter just shrugged again, and sat down next to Lily's father, loosening the silk scarf he had tied around his neck as a cravat, and fanning him gently with one hand. Then he dug out his notebook, and scrawled, *Didn't think. Hate her. Sorry, but it's true. Wasn't going to let her make you like G.*

'I hate her too,' Lily said slowly. It was a strangely helpful thing to say. It ought to be wrong to hate one's mother, Lily thought, but then most people's mothers weren't trying to use them as magical death traps. 'What are we going to do with her?'

Can't he get rid of her? Peter suggested, jerking his head towards Argent.

'With pleasure,' the dragon muttered.

'She's still my mother,' Lily said in a small voice. 'I know I said he could eat her, but I can't just tell him to…'

'I wouldn't need to be told… Choose quickly, Lily. There's so much delicious magic inside her. Dark, like that chocolate Daniel brought for me. Strong, and a little bitter. Hurry up, do.'

Lily looked frantically around the stage. If only her father or Rose or even Georgie could help her decide, but all three of them were unconscious, wiped out by the power of the magical duel. Daniel had gathered Georgie into his arms, and he was gazing down at her worriedly. Now that the stagehands and some of the performers were starting to creep back onto the stage, he directed some of them to carry Rose and the girls' father to their rooms. There was no older magician to ask. She would have to decide for herself.

Lily watched Princess Jane leaning anxiously over Rose, with a little bottle of smelling salts in her hand, and frowned. The princess had been shut up at Fell Hall for so long. That was what you did with people you wanted to get rid of, but couldn't bring yourself to kill. You locked them up, for ever and ever.

Even that seemed horribly cruel, and Lily rubbed her hands wearily across her eyes. Wouldn't it be better to be dead? But then, her mother had killed so many people. Lily's own sisters. Georgie, almost. Perhaps it was right to be cruel.

Henrietta nudged her leg lovingly, and Lily picked the dog up, rubbing her cheek against the velvety fur. 'I don't know what to do,' she whispered.

'I don't have any good ideas,' Henrietta admitted reluctantly. 'Not very good ones, anyway. I don't suppose we could send her back to Merrythought somehow? And shut her up there?'

'Maybe...' Then Lily suddenly hugged her tighter. 'Merrythought! Henrietta, like the picture! The one I took you out of! Look...' She hurried to the back of the stage, with Peter following her, and Argent swinging his head round suspiciously to see. 'This canvas flat...'

The ballet scene was a romantic one, based on the story of the Sleeping Beauty, with some new music by someone whose name Lily could never remember. The scenery was a riot of roses, spreading over a palace, cleverly painted so that the stone walls and towers seemed almost solid, stretching back into the airy nothingness behind the stage. Lily stood below one of the new flats, canvas stretched over a wooden frame to hold it up, and pointed. 'There, in the window, do you see?'

'No,' Henrietta said flatly, staring at the dark opening painted into the stonework. 'There isn't anything there!'

'But there could be... Argent, do you see what I mean? I brought Henrietta out of a painting with my first spell, I tried to draw her, and she came out of the painting to me. Does it work the same way to put someone *into* a painting?'

The dragon sighed gustily, sending ribbons of smoke twisting up around the empty window. 'I suppose it could,' he admitted. 'I like it... Not as much as eating her, admittedly, but it has a certain charm.'

'You're going to paint her into my scenery?' Daniel asked, staring at Lily's mother in horror.

'If we can work out how,' Lily agreed.

'But we reuse these flats, Lily. We paint over them. It won't be a tower scene for ever.'

Lily chewed her bottom lip. 'I think that whatever you paint, she might always be there. Please, Daniel. I don't know what else to do with her. I know it seems awful to shut her up in a painted prison, but she'll have the shows to watch, at least.' Lily gave a half-hysterical little giggle, and Peter scowled at her anxiously.

Henrietta, who was far less patient than he was, just

bit her, nipping sharply at her ankle. 'Stop it, Lily!'

'Sorry...'

'You can do it,' Daniel said reluctantly. Gently, he passed Georgie over into the huge arms of Sam, who built the sets. 'But if she starts jinxing the dancers, I'm burning that flat. Got it?'

'I wouldn't tell them,' Henrietta suggested. 'You're all superstitious enough as it is.'

'Hurry then,' Argent growled. 'She's flickering – I can feel her magic waking again.'

Lily ran to the pile of paint pots and brushes, and Peter put up the stepladder for her. He and Daniel stood on either side of it, holding it steady, as Lily climbed up, balancing herself on the top of the ladder and trying not to wobble. She had flown on dragonback; how could she be scared when she was only this far up?

'Lift me up there,' Henrietta commanded Daniel importantly. 'I understand these things, being a painting myself. She needs me to help.'

Henrietta wedged herself around Lily's feet, peering at the black canvas, as Lily tried to drag the magic out of her bones. It seemed sunk deep inside her, after the fight. She felt drained and achy. But this was her chance to protect Georgie, and herself. She had to get it right. Closing her eyes, she tried to remember those miserable years back at Merrythought, hiding as her mother stalked past. Georgie's terror as the spells began to take hold of her. The way Mama had sent Marten after them, to drag them back. She felt her magic stir sluggishly inside her, and gripped a paintbrush tightly, begging for this to work.

'Keep still, little one,' Argent murmured. 'Don't fall. There, is that better?'

Lily glanced down and saw that he had dropped her mother, keeping her pressed under one massive clawed foot. Now he twisted his long neck around so that his head was next to the ladder, and his huge, glittering black eyes were gazing into hers. She felt a sudden swooping surge, like those strange dreams she'd had when she was smaller, when she'd been sure she could jump down the main staircase and float. The power of the dragon magic that Argent breathed over her made Lily dizzy, but it was a wonderful, exciting dizziness that made everything seem possible.

The paintbrush was hanging slackly in her fingers, but all at once Lily felt it twist and shiver, and Peter let go of the ladder for a moment to pass her up a pot of paint. He looked confused, as though he thought someone had asked him to do it, but he didn't know quite who.

Lily dipped the brush into the paint and touched it

to the canvas, and then it seemed to take on a life of its own, darting madly here and there. 'Colours...' Lily muttered. 'It needs colours.' She thought of her mother's dark hair, and rust-red dress, the creamy paleness of her skin, and felt the brush falter in her hand, confused. Then she remembered the paintbox – it must have belonged to some long-ago Powers girl, being taught pretty watercolours in the schoolroom. She had found it shoved to the back of a shelf, covered in dust, with its catches rusted and the little tubes all dried up, just the merest smudges of colour around the lids. But she remembered the names. She had spent days chanting them to herself. Starved of magic as her mother lavished it all on Georgie, she had thought they sounded like a spell, even then.

'Alizarin crimson, Chinese white,
Lamp black, Viridian,
Scarlet lake and Sophie's yellow,
Caput mortem...'

Lily chanted on and on as she felt the brush dance in her fingers. A delicious warmth was stealing over her, the sense of a complicated spell working as it should, and she shoved the knowledge of what it was doing to the back of her mind. She could not care, couldn't falter. It would spoil the spell. 'Caput mortem...' she snarled. One of the scene painters had told her that it meant death's head, because it had once been made from ground-up bodies, ones that had died thousands of years ago and been wrapped in bandages to preserve them. Mummies, he had said they were called, almost like Mama... She didn't believe it, quite...

'Caput mortem,' Lily growled out, forcing the brush over the canvas, feeling it fight her. 'Lemon. Violet. Permanent rose!'

What had Mama done to Rose? She must keep on... however hard it was to condemn her own mother to a painted prison.

'Hooker's green, Indigo, Aureolin... Ultramarine!' Lily shivered, and shook herself, and dropped the paintbrush. She swayed on the top step of the ladder, and Henrietta yelped, and then she stopped falling, caught in the talons of the dragon who was watching her spell.

'Where's Mama?' Lily whispered, looking down anxiously. He had caught her with the same foot he had been using to hold her mother down. 'You didn't let her go?'

'There, look.' Argent's voice was a satisfied rumble. 'Your spell worked. I still say she would have been better eaten, but it was a good spell, Lily. Full of deep power.'

'She's there?' Lily asked, twisting herself around his claws to peer up. 'Oh...'

Her mother was standing in the window, staring out across the stage. Lily had expected her to look angry, as though she was about to tear the canvas apart with her nails and fight her way free. But instead her mother's face was peaceful, almost dreamy. Her painted eyes lacked the angry glitter that they'd always had in life, and the hand resting on the stone sill was gently curled.

'She looks *happy*...' Lily whispered.

Argent snorted, a small spurt of flame spitting out of his mouth. 'She doesn't have to fight any longer, does she? You've done well, Lily, I admit.'

Henrietta launched herself from the top of the ladder, into Lily's arms. 'Good. One down. How many more to go?'

SEVEN

Henrietta's words kept ringing in Lily's ears as she hurried along the warren-like passages under the theatre, going between her room, where Georgie was curled small and shrunken into the bed, and her father's, with occasional visits to Rose, who was being waited on by the princess. Princess Jane seemed to be enjoying herself. She confided to Lily that she felt useful, for once, working on some sewing for Maria while she watched over Rose.

Both of the older magicians had woken up, briefly, but they were still exhausted from the battle, too weary to make plans with. Lily had hoped that her father would be well enough to recast the tapestry, so they could try to untangle Mama's spells from Georgie again. But he was still too dazed, and Georgie hadn't woken at all. She seemed to be dreaming, twisting painfully in the bed and crying out. Lily left Henrietta guarding her whenever she left the room.

How many more of the conspirators were there? Their mother had mentioned that there were other 'spell-children', prepared as Georgie had been. She'd even known the Dysart girls by name, the twins Cora and Penelope, who had betrayed Lily and Georgie and had them sent to Fell Hall. She had also said that there was only a little time left. The plot must be arranged for very soon. But they had no way of finding out. Lily felt choked with fear as she scurried about deep under the theatre. How were they going to stop it? What if the attempt on Queen Sophia's life was today? It could be, for all Lily knew. If it went ahead, no one would ever believe that magic could be trusted.

The day after the great fight on the stage, and the painted spell, Lily left Henrietta sleeping next to Georgie, and climbed wearily up to the stage, sitting down on a pile of ropes by the painted tower. The flat was dry now, and it had been stacked up in a pile of others, ready for the performance that night, but Lily could still see the edge of the tower and the window. Her mother was gazing out across the fairyland she was painted into. Lily was sure she could see more than the back of the flat in front.

'I don't suppose I should talk to you, really...' she murmured. 'In case it gives you ideas. But Daniel's always busy, and so is Peter now.' Daniel and Sam had adopted the mute boy as an extra member of the stage crew, once Lily's father had shown them how cleverly he scribbled sets and gadgets in his little notebook. Now he was constantly running after Sam, with all the tools that Sam hadn't realised he needed. 'Besides, it's hard sometimes, when he has to write everything down. It makes him always so serious. I wish I knew what to do next. You said there was only a little time.' She looked up at the stripe of pale, calm face that she could see. 'You know what's going to happen, don't you? No one else seems to understand how important it is... We don't have time to wait, we need to work out the rest of the plot. But I don't know where to go next. Ohhh!' Lily groaned angrily, and buried her head in her folded arms.

'Lily!' There was a frantic clicking and scrabbling of claws, and Henrietta skidded across the stage, barging into Lily in her corner. 'You have to come!'

'What is it? Did Georgie wake up?'

Henrietta shook her head briskly, her ears flapping. 'No. She's still asleep. I think she is, at least.'

Lily stood up, shivering, and stared at her. 'You think?'

Henrietta shrugged, suddenly looking very human. 'Her eyes are open,' she said slowly. 'And she's walking, but I don't think she's awake.'

'Walking where?' Lily yelped. 'Show me!'

'I'm trying, I'm trying,' Henrietta muttered crossly. 'This way. She wasn't going very fast.' She set off, sniffing busily as she led Lily into the passageways behind the wardrobe room and the cast dressing rooms. 'Close now. She has got further than I thought she would... Ah!'

They rounded a corner and found Georgie, in her threadbare nightgown, pulling at one of the doors that led into the alley outside the theatre.

'Georgie, where are you going?' Lily asked, hurrying up to her. She tried to take Georgie's arm, but her sister ignored her entirely. It was as if she didn't even feel Lily touching her. She just kept pulling at the bolts on the door, shaking them and running her hands over the massive keyhole. Lily squashed herself against the door so she could look at Georgie's face. Henrietta had said that she was still asleep, but Lily didn't see how she could be. She'd just bump into things, surely. She remembered Georgie wandering the passageways at Merrythought in a dreamworld of her own magic – she had always looked pale, and pinched and far away. Henrietta had just mistaken that for sleep.

But when she looked into Georgie's eyes, there was nothing there – no life, no sight.

'See?' Henrietta said grimly. 'She's still asleep. Or unconscious. Whatever you want to call it.'

'She's trying to get out,' Lily said quietly. 'Where does she want to go?'

Henrietta peered up at Georgie, who now had both her hands pressed against the keyhole. She seemed to be trying to understand what it was. 'It isn't her, is it? It's those spells. Where do *they* want to go, that's the question.'

'It's starting, then,' Lily whispered. She didn't want to say it out loud – they were talking about treason, she had to whisper, even though there was no one else around. 'The plot. The spells are making her do things.' She patted the door miserably. 'They've got a purpose and they're *steering* her.'

'Don't talk about me like that,' Georgie said grumpily, and Lily gasped, swinging round to stare at her.

'You're awake!'

'Why am I out here in my nightdress?' Georgie had suddenly realised that they weren't in their room, and she looked about her in horror. 'Lily, what's going on?' Her eyes widened. 'Mama! Mama is here! She's coming, isn't she? We have to hide. Or fight. I don't think I can fight her, Lily!' Her eyes began to roll back in her head, eerily showing the whites, and Lily shook her.

'Stop it! You've forgotten.' Lily swallowed a deep breath. 'Georgie, you've been unconscious ever since yesterday morning. When Mama was coming, you couldn't control her spells, and I helped you sleep, so you couldn't hurt us, or help Mama.'

Georgie stared at her fearfully, then she clutched Lily's arms. 'So you're all right? You're safe? What happened?'

'Show her,' Henrietta grunted. 'She won't believe you otherwise.'

Lily nodded, and took Georgie's hand. 'Come and see. Father and Rose were hurt – struck down by Mama. She had these great bursts of magic, they were incredible. She kept taunting Father, saying he'd never hurt her, and at first he couldn't bring himself to. I think he was about to in the end, but she got him first. And then she put a spell around me that pulled all Rose's power out of her, when she tried to protect me. Mama's magic – it was sneaky. Mean, I suppose. Strong as well, but she used how we felt to help her. And we let her do it.'

'*Was?*' Georgie asked, in a small, hopeful voice. 'You mean, it isn't any more? Lily, did you win? How could you have done?'

Lily shrugged. 'We've got a dragon, haven't we? We had to fight without him at first, because the space was so tight – he was too close to grab at her without hurting us. But when she attacked Rose and me, he got so angry, and Mama had pushed us both away with the strength of her spell. So he caught her.'

Georgie went even paler, if that were possible, and her eyes glittered. 'Did he eat her?' she whispered, with a sort of horrified fascination.

'No, because little Miss Soft-hearted here wouldn't let him,' Henrietta muttered. 'We're stuck with her for ever, look.' She trotted between the stacked flats, and Georgie followed her, wide-eyed.

'This is your magic, isn't it?' she murmured, as she stared at the painted figure. 'It smells of you, Lily. I can feel you in it. This is amazing. It's so strong.'

'It was my spell, but Argent helped,' Lily admitted. 'It wasn't all me.'

'Still...' Georgie stepped back putting an arm round her shoulders. 'You're so much stronger than I ever was.'

'That's why your mother was going to pull the spells out of you and put them in Lily.' Henrietta's voice echoed from between the flats, and Georgie went rigid.

'Is that what she said?'

'Mmm.' Lily glanced anxiously at Georgie, wondering how upset she would be.

'Even though she knew it would probably kill me?' Georgie demanded.

'She thought it might kill Lily too. She said she didn't have a lot of time.' Henrietta poked her head around the painted canvas. 'So that's why you're starting to go a bit crazed, I should think. It's all happening. The spells are working up to what it is they have to do.'

Lily glared at Henrietta. She really had no sense of tact at all. Lily was never sure how much she was doing it on purpose.

'I'm not crazed,' Georgie said, but she didn't sound very sure. She glanced at Lily. 'Do you think I am?'

'You were wandering around in your nightie, trying to open a locked door with your fingers,' Henrietta pointed out. 'And your eyes were all wrong. You looked quite crazed to me.'

'You're awake!' Daniel was standing at the edge of the stage, with his arms full of handbills. 'Are you all right?' he added shyly, realising what Georgie was wearing, or not wearing, and staring very firmly at his feet.

Georgie blushed scarlet. 'I must go and get properly dressed.'

'Oh, no one cares!' Lily rolled her eyes. 'We found Georgie sleepwalking,' she explained anxiously to Daniel. 'We think the spells have had some sort of signal, something that makes them start controlling what Georgie does. They've been woken, and they're working now. The plot's getting under way. Unless it was just Mama being close again.'

'It doesn't feel like that,' Georgie murmured. 'I almost remember what I was doing. I had to get somewhere. A house. Not far from the river.'

Lily turned to her eagerly. 'But if you can remember where, then we can find the other people in the conspiracy! We can stop them!'

'A whole gang of magicians, all probably as powerful as your mother?' Daniel asked doubtfully. 'How are you going to do that? Without flying that dragon through London again?'

'I can't remember where it is...' Georgie said slowly. 'A tall, white house. Lots of other children. I knew, when I was asleep.' She shivered. 'Maybe I shouldn't sleep now. I can't risk it.'

'Or you should, so we can follow you,' Lily pointed out, and Georgie shuddered convulsively.

'Hang on.' Daniel stared down at the stack of

handbills he was carrying, looking at them as if he were seeing them for the first time. 'Look.' He held one out to Georgie and Lily.

'What?' Lily asked, reading it, and frowning. *Special Jubilee Performances. Patriotic Display. Live horses on stage! Dramatic Tableaux!* 'Where are you getting horses from? We don't have any horses.'

Daniel looked slightly shamefaced. 'A mate of Sam's has a pony, and he says it'll be all right to borrow it. We'll just have to keep it away from him over there.' He nodded over at Argent. 'Anyway, that wasn't what I meant. It's the jubilee. Don't you see? Queen Sophia's Golden Jubilee. Parades. Special appearances. That pageant thing on the river. She's got to be there, hasn't she? They can't palm that off on that mad old mother of hers, even if the queen is ill. She's got to be on show.'

'Oh...' Lily gazed at him, her eyes widening. 'And so everyone knows where and when the queen will be outside the palace.'

'Exactly.' Daniel nodded. 'Thousands and thousands of people. The perfect cover for an assassination attempt, I'd say.' He looked over at Georgie, went scarlet and stared at his shoes again. 'Three days' time. That's when it is. We just have to keep you safe for three days, that's all. And it'll all be over.'

Georgie smiled tremulously, but Lily shook her head. 'No! We can't just leave them to get on with it! It's all very well protecting Georgie, and protecting other people from her, but it's not enough! We have to stop the others too, if we want any chance of bringing magic back to the country.' She caught Georgie's hands. 'We have to, don't you see? If we save Queen Sophia, she'll listen to us, she couldn't not listen.'

'What if she doesn't?' Henrietta asked, very seriously for once.

Lily sighed. 'Then we'd have to go and live somewhere else. America, maybe.'

Henrietta sniffed. 'I suppose. But not in that disgusting lodging house again, Lily.'

'If we don't save her,' Lily added quietly, 'I think we'll have to go to America anyway. I don't want to live here, with people like Mama and Jonathan Dysart in charge. Magicians who think they can do whatever they like, to whoever they like. Jonathan Dysart's spent his whole life pretending not to have magic, just to get himself made one of the queen's closest councillors, so he can turn on her. He'd do anything.'

'Even turn his daughters into weapons, like me,' Georgie muttered. 'I wish I knew what it was I was going to do. I feel like if I knew, I could at least try not to do it.'

'Your father might have an idea,' Daniel suggested. 'Peter said he was awake.'

'Wouldn't he have told us already, if he knew?' Lily said, sounding surprised.

Daniel shrugged. 'It depends. He's your father – he might not want to tell you something that would frighten you.'

'Exactly.' Their father's voice was threadlike, as he stumbled out onto the stage, leaning on Peter's arm. 'I could feel you thinking about me.' He smiled at Lily's round eyes. 'Yes, it's a useful little charm.' Then the smile faded as he looked at Georgie. 'I didn't want to tell you what I suspected. I couldn't... But you're right. It's better to know.'

'To know what?' Georgie demanded sharply.

'The spells will kill you, as well as Queen Sophia,' her father told her simply. 'It would make the magic much, much stronger. You would be a sacrifice, you and all the other children.'

'They'll all die?' Lily asked, feeling suddenly sick.

Her father nodded. 'I suspect so. I'm not absolutely certain, of course. There may be some other edge to the spell.'

'Then all those magicians have been bringing up their children, teaching them the spells, just knowing that they're going to die at the end of it...' Lily shivered.

'That's horrible. But I suppose it isn't so different from the other spells you've used,' she added slowly to Georgie. 'They all feed off you. The wolf spell stole your blood. And so did the spell you started to do yesterday – the one that was supposed to make me do everything you wanted.'

Georgie nodded. 'Oh. Yes, I do almost remember... Do you think Cora and Penelope know what they're doing?' she asked, frowning. 'Unless their spells aren't the same as mine. I can't see those two agreeing to be sacrificed. When we met them at Aunt Clara's house, I didn't think they were like that at all.'

Lily shook her head. 'No. They'd want to be part of the new state of things afterwards. Magicians lording it over everyone else.'

'Exactly,' Georgie agreed.

Peyton Powers sighed. 'The spell would be stronger if they actually chose to die themselves, for love of the cause, but that's hard to teach.' He smiled at Lily, but his eyes were shiny with tears. 'Not everyone is as brave as you. I don't think those children know what's going to happen. They've only been told that they're part of something wonderful.'

'Like you were,' Lily said sadly to her sister.

Georgie looked at her thoughtfully. 'Maybe we ought to tell them?'

Lily blinked at her. 'Cora and Penelope? They betrayed us, Georgie! They betrayed us to the Queen's Men! It was those two little demons that got us sent to Fell Hall.'

'Well, to be fair, we did want to go there anyway,' Georgie pointed out. 'We wanted to find out about the magicians' prison. And we had to rescue Peter.'

'They didn't know that, though,' Lily said stubbornly. 'And it was their own plot that they were betraying too. They were so desperate to be the special ones who brought the magic back, they couldn't bear the thought that it might be you that killed the queen instead.'

'He didn't want to send you there, you know. Their father,' Henrietta put in. 'I heard him telling them so, while the officers of the Queen's Men were taking you away. I was still knocked out by those deadening spells they were throwing around, but I could hear, even if I couldn't move. He was furious. He said it was a waste of your magic, and you were too valuable to send away to Fell Hall, but now he had to, because it would be too obvious to let you off.'

'You never told us that!'

Henrietta shrugged irritably. 'There was quite a lot going on, Lily. I had to chase a carriage all the way out of London, remember? It didn't seem all that important at the time.'

Lily stroked Henrietta gently, remembering her bleeding paws. 'Sorry.'

'So, he knows how the magic will be used...' their father murmured. 'All of you together. He didn't want to waste you.'

'They probably wouldn't believe us, anyway,' Georgie said thoughtfully. 'I wouldn't believe me either. The way they spoke about their father, I think they loved him. Imagine how it would feel, to find out what he was going to do...'

'Maybe they won't ever have to know,' Lily said uncomfortably. But she wasn't sure how that could be true.

EIGHT

'What are you reading?' Lily asked, peering over Peter's shoulder.

Peter sighed and passed her the newspaper, and went on munching the doorstep of bread and cheese that was his lunch. He had gone out and bought it himself, Lily knew. He quite often fetched something for Daniel and Sam and some of the stagehands as well – most of the shopkeepers close by knew him, and they were happy enough to read a note. Lily was pretty sure that Peter couldn't care less what people said, anyway. It was easier for him to ignore stupid comments, he could just look away, instead of having to try not to listen. But even if he understood what they said, he was still spending his own money, his wages, from a job that he'd chosen and he loved.

Whatever happened, Lily thought ruefully, at least she'd rescued Peter. Only a few months ago, she'd thought he would live and die at Merrythought – as she would.

'Oh... A jubilee pageant.' Lily sighed. 'The jubilee's only two days away now, and we still don't know anything about the plot.' Georgie hadn't had another sleepwalking episode. Lily wasn't sure if she was trying to hold the spells back – maybe without even knowing she was doing it. But she had slept quietly the previous night – after Lily had lain next to her for more than an hour, feeling her wriggle, and turn this way and that, too scared to close her eyes. After Georgie had finally given in to sleep, Lily watched her in the darkness for what felt like half the night. She wasn't sure if she wanted Georgie to walk, or not.

Lily rubbed her hands across her eyes wearily. 'I don't know what to do. I was even wondering if we should try and go to the palace, and talk to someone. We could warn her...'

Peter stared at her, his eyes wide and dark. He shook his head sharply.

'Oh, I know.' Lily sighed. 'But we have to do something. I hate waiting like this. I feel as if I've got ants pattering about all over me. And inside too.' She shuddered. 'My magic's crawling with them.' She flapped the newspaper at her face irritably. Then she held it out in front of her and squeaked, her eyes widening. 'Look!'

Peter took the paper, and stared at the picture Lily was stabbing her finger at. A group scene, very carefully staged, of six girls, mostly about Lily's age, although one was older than Georgie, she thought. About the age her sister Prudence would have been, if she'd lived.

But it was the two girls in the centre, staring seriously at the photographer, who'd made Lily cry out. Their long dark curls were beautifully arranged to cascade over their shoulders, and even in the smudgy, feeble print of the newspaper, their eyes looked glassily strange.

They were green, those eyes, when one saw them for real. Eerily green, shining out of their creamy-pale faces like lamps. Cora and Penelope Dysart, Jonathan Dysart's twin magician daughters.

Henrietta growled at the picture, baring her teeth.

'Those are the girls who got us sent to Fell Hall,' Lily explained to Peter. 'The Dysarts. Daniel was right, the jubilee procession is the perfect chance. If Cora and Penelope are part of the pageant, that must be when it's all going to happen. This proves it, don't you see? The pageant is just to get them close to the queen.

I should think all of these girls are magicians.' She scanned the article quickly. *A masque to glorify Queen Sophia – one of the many wonderful scenes and spectacles designed to celebrate the fifty years of her reign. Children of prominent citizens.* Lily gave a little snort of bitter laughter. Prominent secret magicians, more like. Jonathan Dysart must have taken it on himself to choose the children.

'Perhaps we should go back to their house – they live next door to Aunt Clara and her family, you see,' Lily explained to Peter. 'We might be able to find out something...' But it seemed a very thin sort of plan, and Peter shook his head doubtfully.

Your aunt would hand you over to the Queen's Men if she saw you, though, wouldn't she? he wrote.

Lily nodded. 'I could borrow your spare jacket,' she suggested hopefully. 'Dress as a boy. I bet they wouldn't notice me then, just loafing about. I could hold horses for people,' she added.

You wouldn't know which end of a horse to hold, Peter scrawled, smirking at her.

Lily elbowed him, but it was unfortunately true. She didn't know anything about horses. Except that they were big, and had very big teeth.

'It's the only way we're going to get close enough to find out anything,' she argued. 'I could follow them.

There must be rehearsals for this masque thing.'

Lily! I think it's happening! It was a high, frightened scream inside her head, and Lily jumped up frantically. She stood, turning her head this way and that. It wasn't like hearing someone cry out – she couldn't tell the direction in the same way. She had to hold Georgie inside her, and run to that terrified voice. She grabbed Peter's hand, patting his face to make him look at her. 'I think she's about to sleepwalk again! The spells have got her!'

Then she darted away, hauling him after her, towards the theatre wardrobe. She should have guessed at it first, she realised. It was always where Georgie went when she was frightened, or upset. She loved the gossipy room, full of dancers and seamstresses, with the kettle on the little oil stove in the corner. The only disasters there were people complaining that their costumes had torn, or that they'd lost a dancing slipper.

Georgie was in the doorway, with Maria, the wardrobe mistress, standing anxiously beside her.

'She went strange,' Maria hissed to Lily. 'Her eyes – like a curtain came down over them. And she was talking, then she just stopped all of a sudden.'

'It's the spells,' Lily murmured, staring at her sister. 'She – she isn't herself.'

'My little brother used to walk in his sleep,' one of the dancers suggested, peering at Georgie round the door. 'My mother always used to tempt him with a bit of bread and bacon. Lure him back to bed, you see.'

'But she wasn't in bed,' Maria snapped. 'She just lapsed into it. Should we wake her, Lily?'

Lily shook her head. 'No! No, we want her to stay like this,' she explained, feeling the two women stare at her disapprovingly. 'If we work out why the spells are making her do this, we might be able to stop them, you see,' she added. It was almost true. She trusted Maria, but the fewer people who knew the real purpose of the spells inside Georgie, the better. Maria had a brooch pinned to her blouse, a little enamel crown – they were being sold everywhere, to celebrate the jubilee. However unpopular the Queen's Men were, there was still a deep-seated love for Queen Sophia. Announcing that Georgie had been shaped almost from birth to murder her was not a good idea.

Georgie had been hesitating in the doorway, her head turning slightly from side to side as though she were listening. Now she stretched out one hand, so that her fingertips brushed the wall of the corridor, and set off walking, her pace slow but steady.

'Will you unlock the doors for her?' Henrietta asked, scurrying along beside Lily.

Lily nodded. 'If I have to, but I wouldn't be surprised if – look! I thought so...'

Georgie dipped her hand into the hanging pocket tied to the belt of her dress, and brought out a key. Her fingers clenched convulsively round it, and then she turned sharply into a different passage – one that led to the same side door that Lily and Henrietta had found her by the day before.

Where did she get the key! Peter thrust his notebook over Lily's shoulder, and she turned back to look at him. 'I don't know! She must have stolen it from one of the doorkeepers.' Lily shivered. She hadn't seen Georgie under the control of the spells since yesterday morning, and she thought she'd been watching her so closely. But somehow her sister must have slipped away. The spells were sneaky, she ought to know that by now.

Georgie yanked at the bolts. She seemed stronger than usual, pulling at them fiercely and then rattling the key in the lock. The spells weren't frightened of being heard, Lily thought unhappily. They would be ruthless, if anyone tried to stop them. And they would use strength that Georgie didn't have, and destroy her doing it.

Georgie swung the door open, and set out determinedly down the side street, making for the main road, where the theatre had its grand frontage. Once there, she picked her way unerringly across the street, avoiding carriages and passers-by with an eerie ease. The spells seemed to be seeing for her.

She plunged through the streets, heading away from the shops and theatres towards the parks and smart houses closer to the palace. Lily and Peter followed a few steps behind, with Henrietta trotting beside them, alternately growling and panting.

Georgie kept walking, never stopping to ask the way or look at the street names. She just walked on and on, until she came to a pretty crescent of tall white houses, their doors glossily painted and the front steps all freshly whitened. The crescent looked out over one of the parks, where a fountain glittered in the sunlight, and the whole street looked too smart and perfect to be housing a murderous gang of magicians.

Georgie padded quietly up to the steps of one of the houses and stopped, her head turning in that same odd way again, as though she were waiting for instructions on what to do next. Lily and Peter realised that the three of them were alone in the street – not the sort of street where one could loiter inconspicuously, at all.

Could we watch from the park? Lily wondered. If they hovered at the bottom of the steps for much longer, a smartly dressed footman would probably be

144

sent out to hurry them away. She was sure she could feel eyes on her already. *Perhaps a spell, to hide them?* she thought, dithering.

Peter tugged at her arm imperatively, and Lily swung round to see the front door starting to open. She backed away, expecting the footman, or even the butler.

Instead, Jonathan Dysart stood at the top of the steps, staring down at Lily and Georgie. Lily caught her sister's arm, ready to run. But Georgie simply gazed up at the open door, and began to climb the stairs.

'Georgie, no,' Lily hissed.

'Oh, it's quite all right. You are in the right place. I could feel you coming. The Powers girls, isn't it?' His voice was soft and velvety, and it made Lily shiver. Now the ants crawling inside her seemed to have their feet stuck in honey. It reminded her of Mama's charm magic. Jonathan Dysart reached out to wrap an arm round Georgie, who stared blankly out across the park, and he beckoned Lily with his other hand. 'I was so very sorry to have to send you girls to Fell Hall,' he murmured. 'Those bad daughters of mine. They have not been used to working with other magician children. Though now, of course, all that has changed. Cora and Penelope will be most glad to see you safely returned.'

Lily was willing to bet that they would be no such

thing, but she only smiled, hoping that Mr Dysart had not spoken to their mother in the last few months. That he had no idea they were not part of his foul conspiracy.

'So after the, er, strange goings-on at Fell Hall, you girls have been making your way back to London?' Mr Dysart enquired delicately, and Lily nodded. She didn't want him knowing anything about the theatre.

'And we brought Peter with us from Fell Hall too,' she explained, wanting to distract Mr Dysart from thinking about what exactly had gone on at the reform school for magician children, and how she and Georgie had been mixed up in it.

'Indeed, indeed...' Mr Dysart ignored Peter entirely and looked thoughtfully from Georgie, so white and silent, to Lily, who was clearly not under the influence of any spells whatever.

Lily smiled at him, fear stretching her grin horribly wide. 'Georgie has most of the magic in our family,' she explained. 'Mama never trained me. But Georgie was so certain that she had to be here, and I didn't want her to come alone. May we watch – whatever it is you're doing?'

'Oh, we're just rehearsing.' Mr Dysart twirled his dark moustache, and smiled behind it. 'A little scene to celebrate the miraculous reign of our dear Queen

Sophia. She has been so kind as to promise to watch our efforts on her special day.' He patted Lily's cheek. 'Of course you may watch, little one. And we will find a special part for your dear older sister to play. A nereid, perhaps, with seashells.'

Lily nodded vaguely. She had very little idea what he was talking about. What mattered was that he was turning back towards the open door, and taking Georgie with him. Lily hurried after them. She wasn't entirely sure if it was a good idea or not, but she wasn't letting her sister go in there on her own, and Peter wasn't leaving either of them.

Jonathan Dysart led them into the house, past a strangely blank-faced housemaid, who curtseyed without really looking at them. She looked as bespelled as Georgie, Lily thought. She supposed that the staff had to be, here in London. At Merrythought, the servants hadn't had much chance to betray the family, shut away on the island as they were. And they had been too terrified of Mama to write home with secrets. But if they left the Powers family's service and went back to the mainland, she addled their memories before they went.

Lily was too anxious to take much in as they followed Mr Dysart up the stairs, but the house had a very different feel to Merrythought. It was a light, bright place, with pale paint on the banisters, and patterned wallpaper covered in leaves and flowers and birds. One of them, a tiny yellow thing with a black beak, leaned forward to peer at Lily and Georgie as they passed by, putting its head on one side to watch them with a bright little eye. It twittered at the girls curiously, and then all the others set up an excited chorus behind them. There was a flowery scent in the air, too, and Lily decided that this house belonged to a woman, a young woman. She could feel her magic, hanging glittering in the air.

She felt envious for a moment, imagining how it would be to have a house full of pretty magical tricks. But then she remembered that poor maidservant, and her blank eyes. The young woman who owned this house, and decorated it so prettily, was part of the plot. She meant to murder who knew how many children.

Lily could hear a hum of conversation as they rounded the top of the stairs, talking and laughter and excitement, which wrapped around her as Jonathan Dysart led them into the room. It ran across the whole front of the house, with tall windows looking out onto the park on one side and mirrors that matched the windows on the other, so that the light reflected and sparkled and bounced around, and the long room seemed even fuller than it really was.

The chatter died slowly away as Lily and Georgie stood in the doorway, and Lily shifted uncomfortably as everyone stared. She had been brought up with so few people at Merrythought that she still found it strange to have people staring at her. It had been different on stage, somehow, where she wasn't really herself. This was very much more frightening. It was a little like their first entry to the classroom at Fell Hall, but there everyone had been drugged by spells, and miserable, and they'd hardly bothered to notice two new girls.

The chattering began again, in quiet whispers, as the children wondered who they were. Lily set her shoulders straight, and stared back. How could she have thought these were like the children at Fell Hall? They were all exquisitely dressed, for a start, not swathed in ugly grey uniforms that never fitted, and they were all, quite clearly, magical. It shone and sparkled out of them, even those like Georgie who had the pale, faint look of the enchanted. At Fell Hall half the children had been there by mistake, and had never used magic in their lives. They'd simply had the misfortune to have looked a little different, or perhaps they'd cried too much as babies, or had mismatched eyes, or a hundred other silly reasons. Even the real magician children had been forced to bury their talent under layers of thick, sickly spells that told them they were evil.

'This is Georgiana Powers, and her little sister,' Mr Dysart explained. 'Georgiana will be joining our performance. Why don't you watch from over there, little one?' He waved Lily over to the chairs between the windows, and Peter took up a position by the door, as though he was a footman who had been sent to accompany the girls across the city. A rather oddly dressed footman, to be sure, but he managed the superior expression very well. Lily tried to assume something similar, but she was too worried. What were they doing, all these magicians? For there were adults, too, sitting watching around the room as she was meant to be. They were just as interested in her and Georgie as the children were.

Henrietta scratched at Lily's knee, and Lily reached down to pick her up. The black pug dog curled up into Lily's lap, and Lily leaned down to stroke her, and whisper, 'Should we let them see you can talk? I told him that I didn't have much magic.'

'Tell them I'm Georgie's then,' Henrietta muttered. 'What are this lot doing? Is it some sort of play?'

The children in the centre of the room were arranged around a chair, draped in golden fabric, on which sat a particularly bored-looking girl, her hair dressed high on her head, with a sort of tiara balanced in it. Six other girls were kneeling around her, holding up their arms in graceful curves – or they would have been, if they hadn't obviously been rehearsing this for a while, and lost interest. Most of them were just whispering about Georgie now. The rest of the children were placed in small groups around them, poised ready to start a dance, it looked like.

'Music, please!' a tall girl in a floaty white dress called, and everyone wriggled, and stood straighter, and tried to look a little more as though they were paying attention. Lily hadn't noticed before that there was a piano at one end of the room, and two boys with violins, and a girl playing a flute. They were all magicians too, she realised, with a thrill of surprise. She had never heard enchanted music before.

'You stand here, and join in with the others,' the girl in the white dress murmured, leading Georgie to a little huddle of girls near the front.

Lily decided she must be the owner of the house – her white dress with its green sash was all of a piece with the pretty wallpaper, and the vases of flowers scattered artlessly around the room. If Georgie had been properly there, she would have been scandalised that the girl didn't seem to be wearing any kind of corset, and not many petticoats either.

'So ridiculous, putting you in now, no one cares about us doing this properly,' the girl muttered. 'Still, it won't matter, I suppose. But just for the look of the thing...'

Cora and Penelope were in this group too, and they glared at Georgie, but she was beyond recognising them. She merely stood, waiting expectantly, gazing out across the park. She seemed to be watching something in the far distance, Lily thought with a shiver. Something in the future, even. Cora was muttering at her, but Lily didn't think Georgie could hear at all.

It only took the first few notes for Lily to realise that the music was the final key to the spell. The bored looks vanished, and all whispering stopped. A new brightness came into Georgie's eyes, something that had been missing for weeks. She stood straighter, like a puppet, pulled up by her strings, and she reached out to join hands with Cora, and another girl with dark red hair. The huddles of children formed into stately dancing circles, moving around each other in an enchanted pattern. It meant something, Lily could tell. The music was pulling at her, begging her to join in, and she shifted uncomfortably in her chair.

'Don't,' Henrietta snapped. 'It isn't right. Strong dark magic. Don't let it pull you in. Look at them all!'

Lily knew she shouldn't let the music sweep her into the circle, but it was so wild, and exciting. Like that moment in the theatre, when the whole audience was caught up, waiting to see how one of their tricks would turn out... She was drumming her fingers against the side of her chair with the beat, feeling her heart thump in time. Henrietta jumped off her lap, growling, as Lily went to stand up.

But someone grabbed her shoulders, forcing her back into the chair and shaking her, and Lily lost the pattern of the music, and stared up at Peter in surprise.

'What did you do that for?' she demanded crossly, rubbing her shoulders. His grip had hurt.

Peter glared at her, and waved at the roomful of dancing children.

Lily swallowed, feeling a little sick, as she watched what she had been about to join. The music still called to her so sweetly, and her magic danced inside her, but she stayed in the chair. Peter couldn't hear it, of course. He didn't have to fight the spell. Lily dug her nails into her palms, and imagined her boots nailed to the floor.

They were dancing faster now, the circles breaking into lines that whirled in and out and round the girl on the throne, while her attendants moved their arms in graceful, powerful charms.

'Where's Georgie?' Lily murmured, her heart

suddenly thudding in a heavy panic. They were moving so fast, and somehow they all looked the same, their faces all eyes and wide-stretched mouths. She should be able to tell Georgie apart from Cora and Penelope, her white-fair hair against their dark curls, and the long red hair of the other girl. But they went past her in a blur of magic, calling something big, and angry, and dark. It surged in the air, and left a dank, dirty taste in Lily's mouth like stagnant water stirred up with a stick. She wanted to run, and race away, but she couldn't leave her sister.

Until all at once the music stopped in a jangle of wrong notes, and everyone shook themselves, coming to, and staring uncertainly at each other.

And Georgie looked across the room at Lily, her eyes dark with panic, and Lily realised that she had no idea where she was.

NINE

The girls had been told that they must be back in two days' time, for the performance as part of the jubilee celebrations. Lily knew that there was no danger that Georgie would forget. Waking out of her spell-dream had left her limp and dazed, and Lily and Peter had to hold her up as they tottered back to the theatre.

'You're back!' Their father, who had been sitting in the crook of Argent's arm, writing a letter, jumped up, nearly flinging ink all over the dragon. The ink pot miraculously turned over, and the cap shut with a sharp little snap. Argent shook himself grumpily.

'So what happened?' he asked, in a rather sleepy growl.

'Are you all right? You should have woken me, not

gone chasing off after her, Lily! I only woke up a half an hour ago, and when Daniel told me what was happening I nearly choked.' He put his arm around Georgie, who sagged against him, and reached out to pat Lily's cheek.

'There wasn't time. And you still aren't well,' Lily pointed out.

'I'd be even less well if something happened to you two,' her father muttered. 'And Peter. I was grateful you had him with you, at least.'

'Did you find out what they are going to do?' Argent asked impatiently, nudging at her father with his massive snout.

Lily frowned. She had been trying to think it through on their way home, but as they got further away from the pretty white house her memories had blurred and faded. Georgie could remember nothing, except dancing, but even that seemed like a dream, she'd said.

'It was the music...' Lily told them, looking at Peter for confirmation. 'It was such a strong spell, it even called me in, and I don't have any of Mama's magic in me. Peter stopped me, because he couldn't hear it. It couldn't get him.'

They were all mad, Peter scribbled, holding his little pad up to the dragon, who peered at it cross-eyed and shook his head.

'He says we were all mad,' Lily told Argent. 'It was awful, and wonderful at the same time. I wanted to be part of it. But after Peter grabbed me, I could see it was something strange they were calling up. It even smelled weird. I think anyone who hears it will join in – they won't be able to fight.'

'And the more people who join, the stronger the spell will grow,' Lily's father mused. 'It sounds as though they're planning to harness the power of the crowd. Clever. Very clever and nasty. Did they tell you where you'll be?' he added thoughtfully. 'It would help to know. Then we could at least try to build some sort of counter-attack. Or somehow divert the queen, so she never gets to that part of the procession. But these things take planning...'

'And strength,' the dragon reminded him, his rumbling voice very gentle. 'Strength your wife took, before Lily shut her up in that painted tower. You don't have it in you to fight in two days' time, and nor does Rose.'

Mr Powers subsided back onto the dragon's leg, drawing Georgie to sit beside him, and sighed. He did indeed look very weak, as though the terror of discovering that his girls had disappeared had drained him all over again.

'Just you then,' Henrietta muttered glumly, nudging

her damp nose into Lily's leg. 'As usual. And me, of course.'

'And me,' Argent growled. 'I think the time for secrecy is past, Lily. We are unlikely to defeat such a powerful, well-planned spell without making ourselves obvious. We may as well be dramatic about it. And I have a taste for this dark magic now, after I ate away your mother's spells. Perhaps it's time for the world to see that dragons are no fairy tale.'

'I wish it would just happen...' Georgie murmured. 'I hate this waiting.'

It was early morning, and they were sitting in a pool of sunshine in the little yard behind the theatre. Argent had curled himself there ready to take off, and everyone was sitting along his back, between the spikes. Even Rose was there, wrapped in a blanket, with Princess Jane watching her anxiously. Rose and the girls' father were going to scry from the theatre, and watch. They had borrowed a battered old flugelhorn from one of the musicians, and Peter had polished it to a mirror shine. Rose had shown them that she could see things in its glowing sides – they had watched Daniel eating black treacle out of the tin in his office, his secret vice. Mr Powers was determined that if the girls were in danger he had to know, so he could help, whatever it cost him, and Rose felt the same.

When the spells called Georgie, Lily and Peter were to go with her again, and Argent would wait at the theatre until the great dance spell began, and Lily called him. She could feel him in the back of her mind, waiting eagerly, like a huge vat of extra magic. It made her light-headed.

'The procession's due to start at ten,' Daniel muttered. He was striding up and down the yard – as much as he could when most of it was full of dragon. He had to turn every couple of steps, or hop over a tail-end. 'It's nine already. So they must want you for one of the later parts, surely, or you'd have been summoned by now.'

'Yes,' Georgie agreed wearily. He had been saying things like this for hours, it felt like.

'So perhaps the presentation of the troops out at the Artillery Field?' He frowned. 'Although surely they wouldn't want to have all those soldiers around. It would just be stupid. And I can't see the Queen's Council agreeing to a dance there, it would be too odd... But after that there's only the ceremonial procession down the river. The queen will be on the royal barge, she won't be close enough to any masque you're doing for it to matter, surely.'

'We don't know, Daniel,' Georgie snapped. 'I don't

know when I'm going to do it! Just stop talking about it!'

'But I have to know!' Daniel hissed back at her, grabbing her hands. 'How am I supposed to come and fight for you if I don't know where you'll be?'

'You aren't coming!' Lily told him, gaping. 'You haven't any magic, Daniel, you won't be –' She had been about to say, *You won't be any use,* but she stopped before she got there. It would have been an unforgivable thing to say. Instead she just stared at him, and at Georgie, whose eyes were full of tears as she gazed into his.

'When did that happen?' Henrietta muttered. 'I swear I only turned my back for a minute.'

'What?' Lily turned herself away from the pair of them. There was something magnetic about the way they were staring at each other.

'Them! Look at them, they've gone sweet on each other.'

Lily glanced back doubtfully, and noticed that Georgie had put her hand over Daniel's, and she was crying. Again.

'Well, at least she'll be provided for, if we make it out of this with whole skins,' Henrietta said, matter-of-factly.

'She isn't old enough to have a sweetheart,' Lily

whispered, glancing worriedly at her father. But he was only smiling at them rather sadly.

'She's nearly fourteen, isn't she?' Henrietta shrugged. 'Daniel's only three years older. It'll stop all those ballet dancers setting their caps at him, at least.'

'And maybe that red-headed juggler will stop mooning around after her,' Argent rumbled.

Lily blinked. She seemed to have missed all this. But then she'd had more important things to worry about.

'Georgie?' Daniel was still staring at her sister, but his foolish smile had been replaced with a look of panic. 'Lily, she's not right!'

'Is it happening?' Lily leaned around the spikes on Argent's back to stare into her sister's face. She shivered. Georgie's eyes had gone shallow and silvery, like mirrors, and all the expression had been wiped out of her face. She slipped carelessly down the dragon's side, landing perfectly as the magic took over, and marched away across the yard. They had left the little back gate unlocked – she had to get out, so they might as well make it easy for her, they'd reasoned.

She yanked it open and disappeared out into the back streets, and Lily tucked Henrietta under her arm and hurried after her, quickly kissing her father goodbye.

'Remember that tapestry spell,' he called after her.

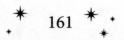

'It's only a thread, Lily. One thread woven through her. We must be able to save her, I'm sure we can. *You* can...' he added quietly, his voice full of disappointment.

Lily nodded, but the tapestry didn't make her think of one dark thread. It doubled over on itself, over and over. The blackness had been spread throughout the whole of Georgie's story, and they'd half killed her trying to wrench it out.

Daniel and Peter followed Lily as she set off after Georgie, making that same journey back towards the white house, though today the streets were full already, with everyone dressed in their best, ribbon rosettes pinned to their coats.

'Wait outside the house,' Lily told them, as they hurried past a crowd of smartly dressed children, buying penny flags from a man with a tray full. 'At the end of the street, maybe. They won't let you in.' She wasn't even sure if they would let her in, today, but no one stopped her as she dashed up the stone steps after Georgie. Several other children were converging on the house, all with that same strange, determined look in their eyes. There was no one guarding the door, and Lily simply followed the others.

'I know where it will be.' Henrietta hissed, as they followed Georgie to the room they had been in before.

Lily looked down at her. 'What? How can you know? Did you hear them say something?' She hadn't heard anything – all the children were horribly silent.

'No. I can smell it. This house backs onto the river. I should have thought of it before, but Daniel said it this morning, don't you remember? The grand procession down the river, on the royal barge. They aren't performing this scene on the riverbank, Lily, they've got a boat, I'll wager you anything. A boat, moored at the back of the house, and it'll draw up beside the queen. And then they'll sink us all.'

'But they'll drown, if they're still caught up in the spell,' Lily whispered back in horror, as they watched Georgie slip behind a screen to change.

'Of course. That's what your father said, isn't it? Those sorts of black spells are stronger if people die, Lily. Even if they don't know they're going to.'

'I read about the boat procession,' Lily murmured. 'There's hundreds of them. So many boats. If the people on all those boats get caught up in the music of the spell, it'll be a disaster.'

'It's much easier to take over running a country, if there's been some dreadful calamity.' Henrietta gazed solemnly up at her. 'People will agree to anything when they're grieving. They've planned all this very carefully, Lily. They'll work their way into power on the back of it somehow, you'll see.'

'No.' Lily shook her head. 'We're going to stop it.'

'Yes.' But Henrietta didn't look very convinced. The children were starting to come out from behind the screens now, draped in brightly coloured tunics, trailing strings of shells and seaweed. Several of the boys were carrying model ships, as though they were going off to sail them in the boating pond out in the park.

Lily followed them as they streamed through the house and out onto the perfectly smooth green lawns that sloped down to the river. Henrietta glanced smugly at Lily as they saw a strange floating platform moored at the end of the garden, with a fussy little steamboat, draped in flags, ready to pull it away.

'They aren't going to let us aboard,' Lily realised suddenly, as they watched the children take up their positions on the barge. Georgie, wearing a pretty rose-pink tunic, knelt in her circle with the Dysart girls, and didn't even look at her. 'If it's on the river, I can't be there, can I? I didn't think of that.' She turned to one of the women watching with her, and smiled, trying to look as natural as she could. 'Please, where would be the best place to go and watch?'

The woman gasped, as though she was trying not to cry. 'Oh – oh, I don't know...' She looked very like the girl with the dark red hair, Lily realised, and she knew what was going to happen.

Lily summoned up an excited smile. 'That's my sister, there. She's so lucky, being chosen to dance for the queen. I do want to see her.'

The mother smiled back at her, a ghastly stretched smile. 'Davenhall Bridge,' she murmured. 'The queen comes onto the barge at Davenhall Bridge.' Then she stumbled away, a lace-edged handkerchief pressed against her mouth.

'The queen comes onto the barge...?' Lily muttered. 'Oh, of course...' The throne in the centre of the scene was empty now, and that girl at the rehearsal had looked so bored because she was only the understudy. They weren't relying on the barge floating near the queen at all. She was going to be right there, in the very centre of the spell.

Lily cast one last look at Georgie, pale and poised on the river, and fled back up the lawns to the house. There had been another barge, this time with oarsmen seated along the front. Jonathan Dysart had been standing beside it, and many of the parents Lily had seen at the rehearsal had been going aboard. They wanted to be there, to see their children dance. Of course they did. Lily swallowed back a sense of sickness. But at least it meant that the house was empty, and no one stopped her as she ran through the echoing rooms and out onto the street, to find Peter and Daniel, and hope that one of them knew the way to Davenhall Bridge.

'I think it's this one up ahead,' Daniel muttered, panting. They had got a hansom cab as far as they could, but the streets were blocked with people, and they had been more than a mile away when they had to start pushing and pleading their way through the crowds.

A low cheer began, rumbling through the crowd, and cries of 'The queen! The queen!'.

'Is it happening already?' Lily gasped. 'How did they get here so fast?'

'Boat full of magicians, isn't it?' Henrietta snapped. She had been kicked several times, and was in a foul mood. They had wasted a good five minutes apologising to the last person who'd accidentally kicked her – she had bitten him back. 'And the river takes them straight here. We had to follow the roads.'

'Listen!' Lily moaned. 'The music, I can hear it starting. We have to get to the front.' She ran forward, elbowing her way through, Henrietta snapping fiercely at people's ankles. A few people pushed back, or shouted at her, but already the music was floating across the water, and they were staring raptly forward, some of them swaying slightly. Lily had thought that the barge would be too far away, in the middle of the wide river, but she could hear the haunting whisper of the flute quite clearly.

'Don't listen,' she yelled, turning back to look at Daniel, and he shook himself, and stuck his fingers in his ears. Lily gritted her teeth, and started to hum the very rude song that the scene painters had been singing the day before – Georgie would be furious with her, she thought, feeling an insane urge to laugh. But anything to keep that music out of her head.

At last she pushed through to the balustrade, and saw the barge floating by underneath the bridge, with the queen's own royal barge close by, the crew pulling back in a sort of floating walkway that they must have used for her to cross between the two boats. They were concentrating hard, Lily could tell, but the barge was drifting, the gilded oars dipping in and out of the water out of rhythm. The music was catching them already.

On the other barge, the queen was seated on the golden throne, cradling one of the model ships. It was meant to be some sort of reference to the sea and the Navy, Lily supposed. All those shells and ships. *Foreign trade and the empire*, she thought vaguely. It must have seemed very sensible. Quite right and proper. But it was all a front.

Queen Sophia was slumped forward, but Lily couldn't tell if that was the spell, or the strange sickness she already had. Lily stared into the whirl of dancers, trying to see Georgie, but she couldn't pick her out, even with that pink tunic. They seemed to be moving too fast, weaving in and out of each other in powerful, dizzying patterns. It was hypnotic, and Lily shut her eyes quickly as she felt the magic begin to seep inside her.

Around her, the crowd of watchers had begun to move in unison, taking hands and bowing gravely to each other, before they set off in a stately swirl, families separated by the spell, even the tiniest children dancing perfect steps.

'Argent!' she screamed into the air. 'Come now! It's happening!' There was no need to call out loud; he would have heard if she had spoken silently. But it helped. It felt like she was doing something.

The dancers on board the barge had changed now – it was a circle, like a whirlpool, with a still centre. The throne. But in front of the queen was another figure, and Lily swallowed miserably as she saw that it wore a rose-pink tunic. All their mama's wishes had come true, and Georgie was leading the spell.

Her sister's arms were stretched out wide, and her face was lifted up to the sky. She was turning slowly, and Lily had a sudden memory of seeing her do this once before, back on the island, when she must have had a rare free moment from their mother's training. Georgie had been smiling then, blissfully soaking in the sun.

Lily could smell that strange darkness again, and the taste of black, oily water was in the back of her throat. It was the riverbank, she realised, the stretch of filthy mud that led down into the deep centre of the river. The water was moving in sluggish swirls around the barge as the magic stirred it up, building it into a dark shell over the dancers, blotting them out completely. Lily wondered if it would simply sink back into the river, dragging the barge and the queen and the children with it, but the water was still turning and twisting, and shaping into something else, something that was growing in the sky above the river.

Lily realised what it was as she heard the solid thudding of wings against the wind, and looked up to see Argent circling overhead.

Georgie was making a dragon of her own.

TEN

Lily reached up her hands to Argent, and the huge silver dragon scooped down one claw to lift her and Henrietta out of the crowd. She could see Peter reaching after her, but she didn't grab his hand. She wanted him with her, of course she did. But this was between her and Georgie now; she couldn't drag Peter into any more danger.

She clambered up into her space behind the dragon's neck, and Argent circled over the river, watching the black water dragon emerge from Georgie's spell.

'That – thing – is bigger than I am,' he told Lily. He sounded rather shocked. But then, it was probably the first time he'd met anything bigger than he was.

'It isn't real...' Lily said doubtfully. It might only be made of mud and water and magic, but it was still there. And it was solid enough to carry Georgie, Lily realised, swallowing painfully. Her sister was sitting on its back, echoing her own position on Argent. 'It's because of you,' Lily murmured. 'That's why she's made a dragon, we made her think of it. The spells use what they can find. Like she sewed the magic inside herself, because sewing's what she loves to do.'

'Is that what I look like?' Argent muttered. 'Except not that ugly black, obviously.'

'Can a water dragon still breathe fire, do we think?' Henrietta asked, trying to sound unconcerned.

Lily glanced down at the swaying mass of people below them. 'I should think it can do anything. It must be made of so much magic. Look how many people there are joined into the spell.' She frowned at the barges, the dancing children, and their parents watching behind. 'Look... It's even catching them, the magicians.' She could see Jonathan Dysart, alone at the front of the barge, spinning in a slow pirouette, his face tipped up to the sky. 'They can't have meant for that to happen. If their magic goes into the spell, it'll make the dragon even stronger,' Lily murmured anxiously. 'Maybe Georgie's stronger than they thought she would be.'

'Your mother put everything she could into her,' Henrietta agreed grimly. 'She didn't hold anything back. And now the spell's taken over everything. That creature's the size of a house. Lots of houses...'

'It doesn't have hundreds of years of experience with those wings though,' Argent said, spiralling down closer to the black dragon. 'I can still outfly it.'

'I don't think it will care about that,' Lily said slowly, as the black dragon opened out its huge, bat-like wings and began to swish them through the air, gaining height incredibly quickly. 'They don't want a flying competition. They just want to destroy the barge. They're going to dive on it!'

'Hold on,' Argent roared, soaring up into the air, underneath the black dragon. The huge creature pulled out of its dive, shooting past them sideways, and as it went by it glared at Lily with sulky, reddish eyes. She could see Georgie, perched tiny and fragile on its back, and she was sure, as they shot by, that her sister was staring out at her in panic.

'It's finished with her,' Lily whispered. 'She's used up.' But her words were whirled away on the wind as Argent flapped fiercely after the black dragon.

'It's turning!' Henrietta howled. 'It's coming after us!'

She was right. The black dragon seemed to have

worked out that it would have to get rid of Lily and Argent to attack the barge. It surged towards them, night-black wings tearing at the sky, and Georgie clinging white-faced around its neck.

'Now it's used up all her magic, it isn't bothered about Georgie any more!' Lily screamed to Argent. 'It doesn't care if she falls off. We might have to catch her.'

'That's not fair!' Henrietta growled. 'He has to hold onto us – and catch her too?'

'Indeed,' Argent agreed in a muttery growl, somehow standing on his back legs in the air, and flailing his claws at the larger dragon. But his claws only skidded away, as if the black creature was armour-plated, and it swung its massive tail around, hitting Argent broadside and sending them tumbling over and over towards the water.

Lily dug her nails into the cracks between his scales and closed her eyes, frantically mouthing a spell that she was making up on the spot, a stupid nonsense of a spell about towels and flatirons and fires and tea that was meant to stop them all drowning. She could feel Henrietta joining in, sending her images of dry fur toasting in the sun, and hot buttered toast, and Great-Aunt Arabel's waterproof raincloak. Lily wove them together in the rushing wind, trying to build a bubble of magic that that would keep them all out of the water.

'Lily, stop it. All I can smell is tea and toast, and it does not help!' Argent howled, pulling out of his dive with his silvery belly skimming the water. Lily wasn't sure if he had done it by himself or if her spell had helped at all.

Still, the sharpness of Argent's talons had scared the dark dragon away, and they had a moment's breathing space while it circled thoughtfully around.

'What do we do?' Lily screamed.

'I don't know,' Argent growled back angrily. 'The spell that made it is so strong – it's enormous, and I don't think it's even worked out that it can flame yet.'

'Let's not tell it!' Henrietta wailed.

Lily shuddered. She couldn't imagine the flames that a dragon that size could produce. It could simply burn the queen's barge. 'I know it's big,' she shouted. 'But you can fly better, like you said. Can't we trick it somehow? Can we tempt it to fly along the surface of the water and make it sink, or something like that?'

'It can probably swim,' Argent muttered bitterly. 'But it is worth a try, I suppose.' He ducked down low, skimming over the surface of the river again, diving close to the barge in what looked cleverly like a protective loop. They were so low to the water that Lily was sure she could trail her fingertips in it.

On the barge, the magician children were still dancing, but they were staggering, and several of them had already fallen. Queen Sophia had collapsed half in, half out of her chair. Lily couldn't even see if she was alive. The rest of the procession of boats had come in range of the spell by now, and they were floating unmanned, their crews dancing and dipping in a strange enchanted hornpipe. As Lily watched, the royal barge, where the rest of the court were gathered, foundered slowly on the muddy bank, and started to tip sideways into the barge of magicians.

'Were they part of the spell?' Lily yelled, leaning down sideways and trying to see. 'Look, their barge is going under! If they haven't broken free from the spell, they'll drown!'

'Good riddance. I can't save them and the queen, Lily, who do you want?' Argent snarled, turning his head to watch the black dragon, making sure it was following him down close to the surface.

Lily twisted round, glancing anxiously between the black dragon and the barges. Ladies-in-waiting were starting to slide into the water, still trying to dance. Lily caught her breath as she saw the old queen, the Dowager who so hated magic, waltz delicately into the water, her stiff silk skirts buoying her up for a moment before she began to sink.

'It isn't deep,' Lily murmured. 'They're nearly at the bank, if only they'd wake up!'

'Help me, Lily!' Argent gasped. He jolted suddenly, almost shaking Lily loose, his wings stalling in mid-air.

'What's the matter?' Lily screamed, clutching frantically at his scales.

He shook his massive head. 'I don't know. Ah! A message...from your father.'

A surge of magic shivered through Lily's fingers where they were pressed into his scales, and she heard the message too. A faint voice, speaking through their ancient family connection to the dragons.

Argent! Lily! The spell! Rose is scrying and we can see the creature, I can see him! He's Georgie's magic. Remember, we pulled away part of the spell!

And after him a sweeter, older voice as Rose joined in. *The loose thread! Find the loose thread!*

Lily turned round to stare at the black dragon, close behind them now. A loose thread, where they had yanked the stitching out of Georgie's magic... Really? The dragon looked horribly whole.

'He must have a weak spot,' Argent roared. 'And let us hope he does not know where it is!' The knowledge seemed to have given him a new strength, and he doubled back on himself in a sudden swift turn that took the black dragon unawares. Argent came clawing and spitting and flaming up underneath him, trailing his tail in the water as he dragged at the dark creature above.

'There! There! It's there!' Henrietta was dancing up and down with excitement, so much so that Lily had to clutch her collar to stop her falling off. 'Under the wing, look! A hole! I can see it!'

Lily leaned out to the side, peering up under the huge creature to see. It seemed so solid, even though she knew it had been made only out of mud and spells. Its wings cracked and thundered above her, and its long neck coiled down, bringing its snaky, wedge-shaped head horribly close. Its eyes burned, and wisps of greenish-black smoke were starting to seep between its jaws.

Then Argent screamed in triumphant rage and lashed his claws at the black dragon's side, scoring down underneath the leathery wing and pulling.

Lily gasped at the sudden stench of raw, angry magic that came tumbling out as the black dragon seemed to suddenly deflate. It sagged like the broken hot air balloon that Daniel had shown them once, caught in the trees in the park. The great black creature folded in on itself and broke apart, just so many scraps of silk.

'Georgie! Catch her!' Lily screamed.

But Argent let out a great, laughing, triumphant roar. 'Look, Lily! We don't need to catch her.'

Lily stared up into the sky, watching the ragged pieces of black silk flutter down and float upon the oily water.

Floating down among them was a girl, a girl that Lily knew was her sister, although she looked so different. Her hair was golden, instead of sickly white, and she was wrapped in a ragged black silk cloak that fluttered around her, bearing her up against the air. And she was smiling, smiling as she stepped down out of the sky onto the dragon's back, and crouched to put her arms around her little sister.

'Has it gone?' Lily gasped hopefully, and Georgie stretched out her arms, flicking her fingertips and grinning.

'All gone. It's only me. No black thread, Lily. No black thread.'

ONE YEAR ON

The bell above the door jingled, and a white-haired gentleman in a lavishly embroidered waistcoat hurried in from a room behind the counter. His hair had fluffed up like a dandelion clock, and it was sparkling slightly, just a faint green shimmer.

'Lily! Sweetheart, you didn't tell me you were coming!' He glanced behind him a little anxiously, back into the storeroom behind the shop.

'Rose sent me with a list.' Lily pulled it out of her cloak pocket. 'She says we need all this, she's doing some special spell for the princess – the queen, I mean.' She still found it difficult to remember. They had spent months living at the theatre with Princess Jane, with her mending their dresses, and fussing because Lily had gone out without a hat, or lost one of her gloves. It was tricky to think of her as the queen now, even though it was a year since the jubilee, and the great fight over the river.

Argent had set Georgie and Lily down on the barge where the children had been dancing round the queen, and they had tried to save as many as they could. But these children had grown up with the spells inside them, weaving in and out of their bones and blood. When the spells had taken over, they had given themselves up to the magic, and only a few had survived the dance. The girls had searched frantically among the little piles, but the brightly coloured tunics hid wasted, withered children, all their life used up.

'Why didn't this happen to you?' Lily whispered to her sister, her tears falling onto a small girl's white cheek.

Georgie wiped the tears away and closed the child's mouth, stroking her hair so it fell prettily around her thin, white face. 'I don't know. Perhaps because all their strength came into me. And I was riding the dragon once the spell grew stronger, I suppose. I didn't keep on dancing. That's what happened, isn't it? They just went on and on until they wore out.' She glanced behind her at the three children they had found alive, now wrapped in the black scraps of silken dragon-fabric, with Henrietta watching over them. 'I hope those three will be all right. They must have held back against the spells, somehow.'

'What about her?' Lily asked, nodding towards the throne, where Queen Sophia lay slumped. 'The dragon didn't sink the barge, and that was how she was meant to die. But she was in the middle of the spell, right at the heart of the dance, and she was ill before...'

She took Georgie's hand, and they walked towards the old lady half falling from the golden chair, the delicate tiara twisted in her white hair. They knelt down in front of her, and Lily felt more tears pressing behind her eyes. They had defeated the dragon, and Georgie was free, but they hadn't won. Sadly, she touched the pale hand, with some idea of sitting her upright. It seemed so undignified for her to be slumped like that. And then the old lady sighed and opened her eyes.

'You aren't dead!' Lily yelped, and the queen almost smiled.

'Not yet,' she whispered thinly. 'That music... Has it gone?'

'It was a spell,' Lily told her, twisting her fingers together miserably. 'A plot. We stopped it, but a lot of people are dead.'

The queen struggled upright, her hand on Lily's

shoulder, and looked around the pretty piles of children and then out across the water. The other barges were back under control now, and the crews were rescuing people from the water. As the queen stood up, a ragged cheer floated across the water, and the crowds on the banks of the river began to wave their hats and clap.

The queen looked thoughtfully down at Lily, her eyes blue and bright and hard. 'You're magicians too, aren't you?'

'Yes.' Lily swallowed. She saw no point in trying to hide. And beside her Georgie nodded proudly.

'Good. Can you make my voice heard across to the banks of the river?'

Lily blinked, and nodded, summoning up the dregs of her magic, and pouring them into the heavy diamond ring on the queen's right hand. 'Hold it up to the light,' she murmured. 'And speak towards it.' The stone glittered as the sunlight caught it, sending rainbow streaks across the silken water of the river.

The queen nodded, and drew herself up proudly, although Lily could feel that she was shaking and exhausted. 'My dear friends,' she began. 'This was a day to celebrate, and it has been cruelly stolen from us. I ask you to be calm, and to be brave. Look after each other. Go home, and try not to be afraid. Do not let anyone tell you to cast blame, or take revenge.' She looked down at Lily and Georgie again. 'Be grateful to these brave children, and feel only pity for these other little ones, whose lives have been stolen for some dreadful purpose. All will be known, in good time. For now I beg you, if you love me, to do as I ask.'

Murmuring voices shivered back to them across the water, and Lily could see that the crowds were nodding and whispering to each other, picking up their fallen belongings and starting to look towards the roads.

'They're going,' she murmured to the queen, and then she felt her shudder, and she wrapped her arm around the old woman's waist. Quickly, she drew the magic out of the ring, so that the queen's sigh of pain would not be broadcast over the water. 'Can you get back to the palace?' she asked. 'We could take you – our dragon could, he would love it, but it's not a comfortable sort of journey.'

'The barge is coming,' Georgie said, 'that big golden one.'

'Good,' the old queen murmured. 'You girls will come back with me. I want to talk to you.'

Lily nodded, and stared up at the dark figure high in the sky. Argent was floating on the thermals, recovering his strength. *We had better bring the princess to her*, she told him silently. *And Father too. He can explain the plot better than we can, don't you think?*

She felt Argent laughing, far above. *I will go now, Lily. Are you sure they will want me in that pretty palace?*

'Can the dragon land in the palace gardens, Your Majesty?' she asked, and felt the old lady tense.

'Indeed,' she said, her voice strictly controlled. 'We will be most glad to receive him.'

When she had discovered that her younger sister was alive, after all these years, Queen Sophia had abdicated almost at once. She had been terribly ill for so long, she had explained, and she was exhausted. She had wished to abdicate before, but there had been no one to rule after her. Since she had no children, Queen Sophia's heir would naturally have been her sister, Princess Lucasta. But Lucasta had no interest in ruling, and spent most of her time travelling abroad.

'Whenever she does come back, we argue,' Queen Sophia had explained wearily to Princess Jane as they stared out across the palace gardens, watching the silvery dragon stretched across the bank of the lake. 'I try to get her to come with me to meetings with my advisors, or a foreign ambassador, and she refuses, and then we fight. She hates the thought of being queen.' The tired old woman looked hopefully sideways at her sister, and Princess Jane sighed, and nodded.

'Someone has to, after all,' she said to Lily and Georgie, as they watched her wander around her old suite of rooms, stroking the little china ornaments on the mantelpiece and running a finger over the face of a tiny, rather battered china doll. 'I shall dissolve the Decree, and bring magic back to our country. Perhaps Rose will consent to be one of my advisors, again. She was my protector once, did I ever tell you that?' She sighed. 'I expect I shall need her. Not everyone will want the magicians here again.'

It had been surprisingly peaceful, though, for such a great change. It had helped, of course, that the Dowager Queen Adelaide had succumbed to pneumonia after her near-drowning. The violence and cruelty of the Queen's Men had made so many people nostalgic for the old times, and without Queen Adelaide's fury, most of the opposition to magic seemed to ebb away.

Now, magic was a part of court life, and it appeared here and there in the streets, like a surprising secret. On her way to her father's shop, Lily had seen a small boy crying over a kite stuck in a tree. It had taken only a moment to send it swooping back to him, its torn tail now whole again, and decorated with small, twittering birds. It was the kind of silly, pretty magic that she had always longed to do.

Lily blinked, and scanned her list again. 'Anyway, I need quite a lot of things. Some very grand person from Talis or somewhere is coming to the palace, and Queen Jane wants them to see that we use magic again now. But nothing too obvious, she says she doesn't want anything flashy. Rose says she's fussing, but then she says that she always did, even when she was a little girl. She liked things just so. We're going to cast the most wonderful spell, Rose explained it all to me over breakfast. Tasteful, but grand, she says. It'll be perfect. So please can I have all this?'

She laid the list down on the counter between them, and lifted Henrietta up to sit on the counter next to it. Her father peered at it and fetched the huge brass scales, and a pile of pretty silken bags in jewel colours. Then he began to climb the shelves all round the shop, pushing around a little ladder on wheels, and fetching down jars. Jars that fizzed when he took the heavy glass stoppers out. Jars that poured smoke. Jars that didn't seem to have anything in them at all, and jars that were full of seething black stuff, and had their stoppers sealed down with wax.

'This is rather a large order, would you like me to send it? Do you need any of it now?' he asked, as he packed the little bags together into a box.

'By messenger?' Lily looked at him doubtfully. 'I'm not sure I'd trust all this to a hired delivery boy, what if he dropped some of it?'

Her father smiled. 'Ah, but I have my own delivery service now. Very fast. Very reliable. The only problem is that he tends to have to deliver through the attic windows – very few houses in London have a garden large enough for a dragon to land in.'

'You're using Argent as a – as a – delivery dragon?' Lily gasped.

Her father shrugged. 'He was bored at the theatre. He says Georgie only uses her magic for the most mundane things, and nothing exciting happens there since you left to be Rose's apprentice.'

Rose had offered to train Georgie too, but Georgie said no. Politely. She'd had enough of magic, she said. It was still there inside her, but she preferred to stay at the theatre and work in the wardrobe. Daniel was trying to persuade her to go back to being his assistant in the illusionist's act, but Georgie said because everyone knew who she was, the audience would just think that she was using real spells.

Even though magic was legal now, it was still quite rare. Some magicians had returned to London, and some had always been there, in hiding, but many more had settled abroad for ever. So magic was rare and exciting, and loved. Brave magicians had saved the queen, and brought back Princess Jane, after all. One hardly ever saw any spells, which meant that Daniel's act was more popular than ever. All the audiences knew that the queen herself had lived at the theatre. Daniel had added a coat of arms and an awful lot of gold paint to one of the battered-looking boxes that were set into the walls of the theatre, and was calling it the Royal Box. He had also added a large sign across the front of the building reading, *By Appointment to Her Majesty.*

Lily thought it was a clever thing to do, even if it was rather cheeky. She supposed she ought to be pleased that Daniel had such a good head for business – after all, she didn't want her sister to be living hand to mouth. Georgie was still claiming that there was nothing between her and Daniel, and that he was far too old for her. But she was almost fifteen, now, and Daniel was only a few years older. Besides, Lily had seen the ring that Daniel kept in the top drawer of his desk. It was in a little red velvet box, and it glittered. She had a feeling that Georgie would like it very much.

'So, Peter is going to build Daniel a mechanical dragon instead,' her father went on, tapping his fingers on the box so that the string coiled itself into a series of tight and complicated knots. 'He's going to design a smaller one that will be able to fly across the stage on a string, apparently. And Argent likes the back room here – good smells, he tells me. I have to say, he is the most marvellous advertisement, Lily. None of the other magic shops in the city – and there are more opening every day, you know – no one else has a dragon living in the storeroom. I don't have the least worry about burglars, either.'

'I ate the last one,' a low, growly voice rumbled from down the little passageway. 'A small bit of him, anyway. Your father made me stop. Peyton, I think your mermaid spell needs attention, it's gone all green and glittery again.'

'Mermaid?' Lily yelped, and her father went red.

'Only a little experiment!' he said swiftly. 'Just research, you know. But at a critical moment, I'm afraid. Goodbye, dearest. I'll be sure to send Argent with your order later!' And he hurried back into the storeroom, quickly pulling a black velvet curtain across the doorway behind him.

'Your father...' Henrietta sniffed, turning her head sideways and trying to see between the curtain and the wall. 'Your father is enjoying himself *far too much*, Lily.'

Lily nodded. 'I know. Mermaids... He and Argent are as bad as each other. I suppose he's making up for all those years locked away without his magic, but I hope he isn't doing anything stupid.' She lifted Henrietta down and they went to the door, trying to listen to the smothered conversation that was going on behind the curtain. Her father was pacing up and down and muttering. By the sound of it, the mermaid spell wasn't working quite as it should. She shook her head, laughing to herself, and then blinked as she touched the brass door handle and noticed the twitching in her fingers. If only she could have brought the ingredients back with her. The way Rose had described the spell was almost mouthwatering, and Lily wanted to start now. Her hands were itching, the magic gathering in her finger-ends.

She would hurry back – perhaps they might be able to start the early part of the spell, at least? Rose had so many little jars and boxes and bags piled up in her rooms in the palace attics, surely there was enough to be going on with?

As Lily eagerly pulled open the door, another girl, much younger than herself, stopped outside the window, staring a little anxiously at the display of glittering jars, and the gilt lettering that swirled across the glass, sparkling in the afternoon sun. *Powers and Daughters, Magical Supplies and Spells, By Appointment to Her Majesty.* She was twisting a wisp of her curly hair around her fingers, as though she was nervous.

Lily smiled at her, and held the door open.

'Is there – is there really a dragon in there?' the little girl whispered, pulling on her hair again. 'One of the boys in my class said there was, but he's always making things up. He said there was a gryphon living wild in St James's Park, and none of us believed that. But then there are such things as dragons. I saw them, two of them, on the day of the jubilee...'

Henrietta stood up on her hind paws, patting at the girl's knee. 'He's there. Ring the bell on the counter.'

The girl's eyes widened to great dark circles as she realised it was Henrietta talking, and Henrietta smirked at her. 'Just don't let them try and turn you into a mermaid.'

'Stop teasing,' Lily told her sternly. 'If you want to see him, I'd go down the road to the sweet shop first, and then offer him some chocolate,' she told the little girl. 'Dragons really are very fond of chocolate...'